A Heart's Journey

MICHELE FLEMING

TATE PUBLISHING
AND ENTERPRISES, LLC

A Heart's Journey
Copyright © 2016 by Michele Fleming. All rights reserved.

This novel is a work of fiction. Names, descriptions, entities, and incidents included in the story are products of the author's imagination. Any resemblance to actual persons, events, and entities is entirely coincidental.

The opinions expressed by the author are not necessarily those of Tate Publishing, LLC.

Published by Tate Publishing & Enterprises, LLC
127 E. Trade Center Terrace | Mustang, Oklahoma 73064 USA
1.888.361.9473 | www.tatepublishing.com

Tate Publishing is committed to excellence in the publishing industry. The company reflects the philosophy established by the founders, based on Psalm 68:11,

"The Lord gave the word and great was the company of those who published it."

Cover design by Albert Ceasar Compay
Interior design by Shieldon Alcasid

Published in the United States of America

ISBN: 978-1-68270-767-8
1. Fiction / Romance / Historical / General
2. Fiction / Action & Adventure
16.04.20

1

August 16, 1863
Chattanooga, Tennessee

"What is the latest, Colonel?" The general asked as soon as the officer made his way into the dimly lit study.

"I received word from Staff Sergeant Clark that there is a Union brigade closing in on the northeast side of town."

"Do they appear to be readying for attack?"

"No, sir. They seem to be only setting up camp at the moment."

"We will monitor the situation for now. Inform me immediately if there seems to be any change. Meanwhile, I will inform General Bragg of the situation. I will let you know if he wants to do anything different."

"General." The officer gave a nod and turned, heading for the door.

From her crouched position on the staircase, Ana could see the officer heading their way and closing fast.

"Hurry, Lucy, he is going to catch us," she whispered as she tried to get her little sister to move. The retreat was not quick enough, however. The man in question witnessed their escape attempt as soon as he turned the corner.

"In the kitchen—now!"

Ana Grace and her little sister stood and solemnly trudged their way to the kitchen, followed by the furious Colonel James Lawson. Although Ana was not able to see his face, she knew it had gone blood-red as it always did when he got angry. Her father made his case as soon as they were in the kitchen and out of earshot.

"How many times do I have to tell you not to eavesdrop? Do you want to get me into trouble?" he growled out in a half-whispered voice.

"No, sir," Ana and Lucy said in unison, keeping their heads low.

Ana swallowed hard in an attempt to keep the tears stinging her eyes at bay. She knew her father would not appreciate seeing them.

"It was my idea, Papa. Don't be mad at Lucy. She wasn't even listening."

Ana felt the need to defend her six-year-old sister, even though she knew her father was aware of her being the instigator. Almost seventeen, she knew better than to be listening in on someone else's conversations. She just couldn't help herself.

There had been so much activity in their home in the past weeks that Ana found herself drawn to it. There were always soldiers coming and going and meetings after meetings. Every day held something new. So for the life of her, she was unable to control her curiosity. The more she heard, the more she wanted to hear.

"The things being discussed in this house of late are very serious and secretive. Our home serves as a convenient headquarters for the army. Therefore, there will be no more disobeying me while they are here. We cannot risk army secrets getting to the enemy, understand?"

"Yes, sir." Ana bowed her head and wiped at an escaped tear. "Papa? Before you go...," she entreated as he was making his way toward the door.

"Yes, Ana."

"I know that the fighting is getting closer to us. I'm scared, and that's why I eavesdrop."

He rushed back and wrapped both daughters in a tight embrace. "I know you're scared. I promise that I will update you each night before bed on as many events of the day as I can, in exchange for no more snooping. But you have to promise me that what I tell you will never leave this house."

"Yes, sir, I promise."

"Me too, Papa," Lucy added.

He kissed both daughters on the cheek before leaving the room.

"Told you, youz gonna git yo'sef in some troubles wid all dat nosey business."

Both girls jumped with fright.

"Liza, you scared the living daylights out of us," scolded Ana.

"You scared me, Liza." Lucy pouted. "That wasn't nice."

Liza gave one of her teasing chuckles and headed their way. It was midmorning, and she was carrying a sack of flour, no doubt getting ready to start the noontime meal. She sat the bag on the counter and then turned back, with hands on her hips, to look at Lucy.

"Maybe it's yo' conscience botherin' ya'," she teased as she looked in Lucy's still-frightened eyes. "You betta shrink dem eyes down a bit, or dey gonna fall right out yo' noggin'!"

"They won't fall out of my head, silly Liza! They're stuck in there."

"Ya neva knows," Liza said as she patted her tiny charge on the head and offered up another chuckle. "Now, you two git on down to da cella and bring me in some a dem snap peas we canned this summa'."

The girls made their way out the back door and around to the cellar. Lucy got there first and opened the door for her sister. Ana made her way down the wooden stairs, stopping halfway to light the lantern as Lucy stomped down behind her.

"Ana, how old was I when Liza came to us?"

"You already know this story, Lucy."

"I know, but tell me again."

"Well, first of all," Ana began as she finished her descent into the deep, dark storage room, "she came here when *I* was a baby, not you."

"I always get that wrong," Lucy admitted. "Daddy hired her to help Mama take care of you, right?"

"Yes…and the house."

"I'm glad he did. I wouldn't like it if she was still a slave and not here with us."

"I feel the same way. I don't know what we would have done without her since Mama passed."

"I wish I could remember Mama." Lucy kicked a pebble into the darkness of the far corner of the room.

Ana reached to smooth the hair from her sister's face, took a deep breath, and turned to continue the search.

It always broke her heart when she remembered that Lucy really had no memories of their mother. She was far too young when they lost her. What hurt even more was that the older Ana got, the more she herself was forgetting. It seemed the harder she tried to remember, the faster the little details were slipping away. It was a struggle every day trying to remember the sound of her mother's voice or the smell of her perfume. She vowed, however, never to give up the effort.

"Here are the peas, Ana." Lucy grabbed a couple of jars and brought them over to her sister.

"Thank you, Lucy."

Ana dusted off the blue glass jars, and they made their way out of the cellar and back to the kitchen. As they helped finish cooking the meal, Ana let her mind wander from her mother to more of Liza's story. She marveled how she made her way from slavery to one of the most important members of the Lawson family.

Liza's master gave his slaves many freedoms other slave owners found unacceptable. He caused quite a stir when he freed all his slaves after his plantation burned to the ground. The rumor was that one of the other plantation owners started the fire as a warning, but no one ever found out for sure.

The majority of the slaves on the plantation stayed to help rebuild, Liza's remaining family among them. She, however, wanted to see more of the world and headed north with a few others and ended up in Chattanooga. She became a nanny to Ana and Lucy not long after arriving. Ana felt truly blessed to have her in her life all these years.

August 20, 1863

"Ana, I need to speak to you and your sister," their father James announced as he entered the girls' room to tuck them in for the night.

Liza began to move for the door.

"You too, Liza. Come, sit here with the girls."

The three moved to sit on the edge of the bed. James began to pace back and forth in front of them. Ana knew he was using this time to weigh his words before he spoke.

"What is the matter, Papa? You look troubled," Ana pointed out.

"The Union troops are getting closer to the city, and I feel it is in your best interest for you to leave town for a while."

"But, Papa—"

James raised his hand to stop her from going on. "I have thought a lot about this and see no other way."

"You said that the troops were only camping out there. They will move on eventually."

"No, honey, they will want to take Chattanooga. They want control of the river and the best supply routes. An attack is coming, and I fear it will be soon. I have contacted your Aunt Josie in Texas, and she wants you out there."

"Texas! That's forever away!" Panic washed over Ana, and she reached out, taking hold of her father's arm.

"It will only be for a short time, my dear. I will send for you once I know that we have full control of the city and there is no chance of another attack. I cannot lose my girls! I am doing the only thing I can think of to keep that from happening."

Ana spoke, overcome with a fresh wave of fear, "What about Liza, Papa? We can't leave her behind."

"I have paid for her to go as well," he announced. Turning to address the woman in question, he continued, "I hope you will agree to this. I trust no one but you to take care of the girls."

Liza took a deep breath, lifted her chin in the air, and said with all the bravery she could muster, "Yes'sa, I will protect 'em wid my life."

"I know you will," James replied with confidence. "You all will be on the morning train on the twenty-second."

"That is the day after tomorrow!" Ana began to cry, forgetting all about her father's aversion to tears.

Lucy began to cry too as she began to see the picture unveiled before her eyes. Hoping to avoid her customary wailing, Ana reached to put her arm around her and pulled her close.

"I know. I have asked permission to have the day off tomorrow so we can spend it together. We will head into town, and I will treat you to lunch at the hotel," he explained with faked excitement, his attempt at changing Lucy's mood. "While we are doing that, Liza will be here packing for the three of you."

"I don't want to go, Papa!" Lucy protested through her tears.

"This will be a great time to get to know your Aunt Josie. Her and your mother used to be close, and I know your mother would be pleased that you are finally going to get to visit her. For now, though, you need to get some sleep. We have a big day ahead of us tomorrow!"

He helped them both under the covers, gave them both a quick tuck, and ended the nightly ritual with a kiss to their foreheads. He straightened his frame and gave a forced smile before exiting the room. Liza sat on the edge of the bed and reached with the hem of her apron to dry the tears rolling from Ana and Lucy's eyes.

"Now, now, li'l ones, things gonna be all right. You gonna see dat'. Try thinkin' of it dis way. You two's gonna getta have a grand adventcha, and I's gonna git ta go wid ya! Girls, we gonna have da time of our lives!"

She bent down over them to add her own kiss to their foreheads and then blew out the lamp before making her way out of the room. Lucy went to sleep soon afterward, but Ana lay there for hours, replaying the whole thing in her mind. She had never been so scared in all her life.

Ana had never met Aunt Josie. Her mother told stories about her before she died, and then her father had talked about her over the years, but she didn't know this lady. Surely, her father was not going to make them go to live with a complete stranger.

So what if she was her mother's older sister? That didn't mean Ana wanted to go all the way across the country and live with her. School was about to start, and she would miss her friends. It wasn't fair! She lay there, stewing, arms crossed and staring at the ceiling until sleep finally took over.

Meanwhile, in the study below…

"Are you sure we can get them out of here safely?" Colonel Lawson questioned his superior.

"Yes, I have no doubts. I informed General Bragg of the situation, and he requested two of his best men to come and see to the task."

"General Bragg, sir? He is not known for his generosity."

"No, he is not," Stone said, smirking. "Apparently it was a good day."

"It is appreciated greatly, I assure you."

"No problem, Colonel. Have a good day tomorrow with your girls and know that I wish them a safe journey. Also, thank that Liza for me. Her good cooking is going to be missed around here," the portly gentleman teased as he patted his bulging middle.

"I will tell her, sir. Thank you."

2

August 21, 1863

THE MORNING DAWNED like any other, and before the girls knew it, they were heading into town with their father. He had promised lunch at the hotel and maybe a stop at Baker's Apothecary for some candy on the way home. Ana and her sister were genuinely excited about their outing despite what was to come the next morning. Their father spent as much time with them as he possibly could when he was at home, but this day was a special treat.

Ana enjoyed every second as they made their way downtown. She listened to the wind in the trees, the sounds of children playing in the hot August sun, and the sounds of the songbirds filling the air. The majestic mountains that wrapped around the city and the winding Tennessee River looked more beautiful to her than ever before. Closing her eyes, she determined herself to memorize every detail.

They made it to the hotel restaurant in time for lunch and sat down to a delicious meal. Lucy kept them in stitches the whole time with her funny stories and the way she emphasized each one with silly faces and sounds. They strolled through town after lunch and stopped from time to time along the way to peer into a shop window or visit with someone they knew. They made it all the way down to where people were gathering in the courtyard of the Missionary Baptist Church. There, James recognized someone and led the girls that way.

"Good afternoon, Captain." James saluted and then shook the other man's hand.

"A good afternoon to you too, Colonel. Well, now, who are these lovely ladies?"

"Captain Marks, these are my daughters, Lucy and Ana Grace."

"Well, it certainly is a pleasure to finally get to meet the two of you."

"It is nice to meet you too, sir." Ana offered her hand and a smile to the man, but Lucy grew shy and hid behind her sister as she always did around strangers.

"Girls, General Bragg has released Captain Marks to make sure you and Liza make the train in the morning."

"I'll be at your place bright and early so we can get you there on time," Marks said, hooking his fingers on his suspenders and puffing out his burly chest.

"Where is the other gentleman?" James questioned.

"Let me get him over here to meet all of you." With a quick nod, he headed off.

"Papa, I wish you could take us," Ana said.

"I don't want to go with that man, Papa," Lucy whined, pleading her case from her hiding place.

"Now, girls, we discussed this at lunch. Besides, General Bragg himself picked these men for the job. I am confident they are up to the task."

From the slightly disheveled look of Captain Marks, Ana wasn't so sure.

"Colonel Lawson, I would like you to meet, Sergeant Jacob Dalton. Dalton is one of our very best men and best dang sharpshooter I've ever seen!"

"It's a pleasure to meet you, Colonel Lawson." The sergeant offered his hand to James.

"Pleasure is mine, Sergeant." James then turned to introduce his girls. "These are my daughters, Ana Grace and Lucy."

"Nice to meet you, ladies."

The smile that accompanied his greeting took Ana's breath away. Thankfully, she recovered quickly.

"You're a soldier?" she blurted out. "How old are you anyway?"

"Ana, such questions are not very polite," her father reprimanded and then gave her a stern look.

"It's quite all right, sir. I get that all the time. I turned twenty last month. And I assure you, Miss Ana, that I am an excellent soldier," he finished with another brilliant smile.

As he spoke, Ana scrutinized the man's tall frame and broad shoulders. She then scanned the front of his gray cotton shirt and down the length of his arms. He had his sleeves rolled up to the elbow, exposing the tanned, firm muscles of his forearms. Tallying his appearance together with his ruggedly handsome, good looks, she decided he would be a real catch if he were not a soldier.

"So, Marks, you and Dalton here need to be at my place in the morning, promptly at 6:00 a.m.," James instructed.

"Yes, sir."

After making a few more plans, Ana and her family were on their way back down the street toward home. Ana couldn't help herself and looked over her shoulder to get one last look at the young sergeant. To her surprise, he was sneaking a look of his own.

They had not gone far when out of nowhere came a loud shrill and then an explosion that rocked the ground they were standing on. Ana could hear the screams of women and children as another shrill and blast filled the air.

"Papa, what's happening?"

"The Yankees! They are firing on us! We have to get you out of here! Now!"

James scooped Lucy up into his arms, took Ana by the hand, and they began to make their way toward home as fast as they could go. Ana looked over her shoulder as they ran to get another look at the town behind them.

Smoke was already pouring out of the top of the candy store along with another building close by. The realization that they had left that store only moments before caused her legs to go weak beneath her.

It was total chaos! People were running around trying to help one another seek shelter. Confederate troops were filing into the area and taking aim at the enemy. Ana cringed as they fired cannons across the Tennessee River. She jumped as explosions signaled they had hit their mark. Ana saw Captain Marks and Sergeant Dalton in the midst of the madness at the same time as her father.

"Captain Marks," James stopped running and shouted over the mounting noise. "Plans have changed! Get to my house as soon as possible!"

As they resumed their hasty retreat, three more loud explosions erupted. Ana couldn't believe this was happening. She looked at her father's face a few times as they ran, drawing strength from the determination and calmness she saw there. As the blasts from the cannons echoed all around, his focus was on one thing only—getting them to safety.

Before Ana realized it, they had made it back to the house.

"Thank da Lord, I thought I'd lost you all!"

Liza wrapped Lucy and Ana in a tight embrace and continued to praise the Lord for their safe return. Liza's praises caused Ana to flash back to a time before the death of her mother and before the mere mention of God in their home turned taboo. The sound of her father's voice broke the spell, however, and she was forced back to present.

"Liza, are you finished packing for you and the girls?"

"Yes'sa," she answered, looking more scared than Ana had ever seen her.

"Then take the girls upstairs and bring everything down."

"Yes'sa. Come on now, girls."

As they reached the stairs, Ana turned and saw her father swarmed by other officers as he headed toward the study. She paused. Her natural curiosity made her want to listen in on the conversation, but the tug on her arm by Liza put her mind back to what they were supposed to be doing.

Once in their bedroom, they got all their bags and placed them by the top of the stairs. Liza then led them quickly back inside and shut the door. She knelt beside the bed and motioned for them to do the same.

"Come here, girls. We needs to pray," Liza said.

"I don't remember how to pray," Ana admitted, but something deep inside her made her want to more than anything.

"I don't know how either," Lucy said through her tears.

"All's you do is talk to God as if He was standin' right in front of ya." Bowing her head and closing her eyes, Liza began whispering her prayer.

Ana realized Lucy was looking to her for instruction, so she decided to follow Liza's lead. She talked to God loud enough so Lucy could hear. Ana listened to the things Liza was saying, repeating as best she could. She asked God to keep them all safe, all the while hearing the explosions in the distance. They stood once the prayer was finished and then made their way into the hallway. Standing at the top of the stairs, they listened, too afraid to go down and possibly get in the way.

The front door flew open. An officer, followed by a couple of soldiers, came rushing in and headed straight to the study. Ana listened as closely as she could to hear the news they had come to share.

"General Stone, sir. We have word the shelling is coming from a brigade led by Colonel John T. Wilder."

"Is that not the same brigade that has been camped out on the other side of the river and to the north for the last few days?"

"Yes, sir. They have sunk two steamers at the landing. We have been firing back at them to no avail. They do not seem to be letting up."

"Let me know if you hear anything else, Major. We cannot let them take the city!"

The door opened again, and Captain Marks and the young soldier came in, in search of James. James realized they were there and came from the study to greet them.

"Are you ready to go, gentlemen? There is no time to waste. I want my family out of here and to safety."

"Yes, sir," Marks confirmed. "The train has been moved to the main track and is sitting on ready, but the Yankees have the railroad cut off to the north."

"Can we get out to the south?"

"If we go now, I believe we can. So as soon as they are ready, we will head out."

James looked toward the top of the stairs and instructed Liza to bring their things down.

"Let me help," the sergeant offered and headed for the stairs.

As he passed, he gave Ana a smile. However, it didn't have the sparkle that it had earlier. In this smile, Ana could see that the recent events were weighing on him.

James called for Ana and Lucy to come to him, and as soon as they reached the bottom, he took them in a strong embrace.

"You have to go now. Captain Marks and Sergeant Dalton are going to take very good care of you."

Lucy clung to her father. "Papa, I want you to go too."

"Are you sure you can't, Papa?"

"Girls, you know it is not possible. The army needs me here."

"Let us stay, Papa, please!" Lucy begged.

"I am sorry, my dear. I will send for you as soon as it is safe." James gave them both another quick squeeze and kiss then stood to address Liza, "Take care of my girls."

Ana was stunned to hear his voice crack and see tears beginning to form in his eyes. She had not seen her father cry since her mother passed. The sight was almost unbearable.

"I most certainly will'sa," Liza said, beginning to tear up herself.

Then her father did something that really shocked her—he hugged that woman.

He turned to Marks and Dalton and addressed them, "Whatever it takes, get them to safety. I don't care if you have to get on the train with them."

"They are in good hands, sir. No need to worry," Marks assured him.

Ana noticed then that Marks was also looking a little strained. He and Dalton then gathered up the trunks and ushered Ana, Lucy, and Liza through the door and down the front steps. A carriage awaited them at the gate, and once inside, Lucy began to cry uncontrollably.

Liza pulled her into her lap and began the task of trying to console her. While Ana, trying her best to be brave, watched her home shrink in the distance. With the sound of shelling echoing all around, Ana's own tears started to fall, and she wondered if she would ever see her home again.

3

THE CARRIAGE BARRELED down the street, hitting holes and dodging other carriages and riders on horseback. Ana felt shaken up by the time they reached the south end of town and the train her father had secured for them. The men jumped out of the carriage and helped them to the ground and then turned to fetch their things.

Ana surveyed the decor of the redesigned passenger car after stepping aboard the train. The car had been fashioned into a comfortable and welcoming sitting room. Ana, along with Liza and Lucy, made their way over to a rose-colored cameo sofa and took a seat. They huddled together like frightened animals, each trying to help one another gain control of their emotions. Marks and Dalton helped them get settled and then turned things over to the conductor.

As they exited the train, however, gunshots and shouting erupted. Dalton came rushing back into the car and began firing one shot after the other out the window. He shouted over his shoulder for everyone to take cover on the floor. Ana fell on top of Lucy to act as a shield, and Liza did the same for her. It was then that Ana realized the train had begun to move.

The conductor pulled a gun himself and began firing out the door. You could hear the sound of glass breaking, bullets hitting and splintering the wooden walls, and the frantic prayers of a tearful Liza. Not knowing what else to do, Ana began to pray as well.

"Please, Lord, save us!" she cried.

The train began to pick up speed, and in a short time, the gunfire quieted. Returning to their seats, Ana and Liza began trying to coax Lucy into calming down.

"Are you three all right?" Dalton asked.

"Yes'sa, I believes we all right."

"Good."

The conductor had been grazed by a bullet, and Dalton turned his attention to him. Liza helped bandage the wound, and then Dalton and the conductor began keeping watch out the windows.

About an hour later, the men agreed they were in the clear and began to relax. By this time, they were well into Alabama and far enough away from the fighting that even Liza, Lucy, and Ana were able to feel more at ease.

Once Ana was sure everyone's nerves had settled a bit, she asked, "Where is Captain Marks?"

Dalton and the conductor exchanged a glance.

"He was shot as soon as he stepped off the train," Dalton explained with a look of regret covering his face.

"Shot! Why did you not help him?"

"There was nothing I could do. He was dead as soon as the bullet hit him, and I had to get you all to safety. I did what I had to do."

Ana hung her head and began to cry again as reality set in. Liza, who was still holding a tearful Lucy, wrapped her free arm around her, and the three of them sat clinging to one another. A while later, tears spent, Lucy announced that she was hungry. The conductor immediately jumped into action.

As he worked, Ana studied him. He seemed to be around the same age as her father, a little shorter and a lot more robust, with dark hair that was graying on the sides. With his black conductor suit, white shirt, and plump middle, he reminded her of a penguin she had seen once in a book of her father's. Ana thought back on the conductor waving his gun and firing off shots and decided the whole scene was rather comical.

"Here you go, little one," the conductor said as he offered Lucy food from a tray he had pulled from the sideboard. "It isn't much, but it's all I could get on such short notice. I planned on stocking up in the morning before we left."

"This is quite all right," Ana assured him.

The tray had several kinds of cheese on it and a loaf of bread. Lucy selected a wedge of cheese, and then the conductor turned and set the tray on a nearby drop leaf table. He went back to the sideboard, pulled out a big silver bowl full of apples and pears, and set that on the table as well. Liza motioned for Ana and Lucy to take a seat at the table and began to help the conductor in serving them.

"Please, Miss Liza, have a seat and help yourself to something," he instructed.

Liza had been a free woman for many years now, but she still would never dream of taking such liberties until everyone else had had their fill. She hesitated until Dalton insisted as well. They each sat in silence while they ate, letting the food and the steady roar of the train's wheels on the track below soothe their anxious minds.

Ana turned her attention to the robust man in their presence. "What is your name?" she wanted to know.

"Oh, forgive me, Miss Ana. In all the excitement, I seem to have forgotten my manners." He stood and assumed his most formal pose and continued with a flourish, "My dear ladies, allow me to introduce myself. Thomas Schneider at your service." He finished with an exaggerated bow that gave Lucy and Ana the giggles.

The giggles spread, and before they knew it, they were all having a time of it. Ana decided right then and there that she liked Mr. Thomas Schneider!

They spent the next several minutes watching him do a multitude of cheesy magic tricks. While everyone else in the car would catch on to the trick rather quickly, Lucy was constantly amazed. Dalton paced back and forth during all of this, stopping every few minutes to peer out a window into the growing darkness. Ana stood and made her way to his side.

"Do you think they will catch up with us, Dalton?"

"No," he began, "I think we're safe. It's a good idea to keep a lookout just in case, though. Please, call me Jacob."

"I'm sorry. I forgot Dalton was your last name."

"That's all right," he said with a grin. "That's all you've heard anyone call me, so it was an honest mistake. When it's not someone from the army talking to me, I would rather be called by my first name, though." He laughed. "That way, I don't forget it."

This made Ana laugh too. He really wasn't like all the other army men she had met, after all. Everyone else was always so serious, especially her father.

"Do you think Papa is all right?"

"Your father's a very capable man. He has the reputation in the army of being very smart and brave. So yes, I do believe he's fine," he said, looking her straight in the eye.

Ana noticed then that he had the most handsome eyes she had ever seen. She couldn't believe she had never noticed before! They were a dark brown with tiny specs of gold around the edges and accented by long, thick lashes.

He then turned his attention back out the windows and removed his hat, revealing a thick mass of dark-blond waves. She watched as he smoothed his tresses back out of his face and replaced his hat. As she studied him, a new and glorious feeling sprang to life within her, causing her face to burn hot.

What are you doing? He is not much older than you, but older nonetheless, and a soldier to boot! She tried to push those thoughts from her mind by changing the subject. "Are you going to go all the way to Texas with us?"

He gave a slight shake of his head. "We will be stopping in Huntsville in a little while, and I am going to try and get a telegram off to your father. I expect him to tell me to leave you in Mr. Schneider's care and then head on back to Chattanooga. I suspect they need all the help they can get."

"Are you not scared to go back? I mean, as much as I didn't want to leave my papa, once all the shelling started, all I could think of was running away."

"It is scary, but I have to remember the importance of what we are fighting for."

"Do you have slaves?"

"No."

"So what are you fighting for then?"

Since Liza practically raised her, Ana had a real issue with slavery. Ana could not imagine someone owning another person. And the stories she had heard over the years about how some owners treated their slaves made her physically ill.

"I'm fighting strictly to protect my home and family. I don't want someone coming in thinking they can do what they want with what is ours or telling us what we can and cannot do."

"So if you wanted to have slaves, then that should be all right?"

"No, that is the one thing I believe is totally wrong. I mean, look at how God helped Moses rescue those who were enslaved to the pharaoh. That's proof to me that no one should be able to own another person and force them to do the work that they should be doing themselves."

His answer satisfied her question but raised a new one.

"You really believe that God helped Moses?"

"Of course, I do. Don't you?"

"I don't know," Ana said with a hint of regret.

"Ana, do you believe in God?"

"I guess I do." The pounding in her heart caused her to wish she had never let the conversation start down this path.

"Tell me what you believe."

"We used to go to church all the time before Mama passed. I really liked going too. I loved the stories from the Bible the teacher would read and the songs we would sing. I even liked sitting during service and listening to the preacher. It captivated me.

"Then Mama took sick with scarlet fever and passed away four years ago. After the funeral, Papa wouldn't allow us to mention anything about the church, or God for that matter. Liza tried to sneak and teach us stuff from the Bible while Papa was away, but he caught her once and gave her a good tongue-lashing. She never attempted it again—not until today anyway."

"What did she do today?"

"She had Lucy and me get on our knees and pray with her before we came downstairs."

"How did you feel in doing that?"

"It made me feel better—not so scared, you know?"

With a smile and a quick tap on her chin with his finger, he said, "I know exactly what you mean."

"Ana," he continued, "don't lose that precious feeling."

"How do I keep from it?" She found herself genuinely wanting to know.

"Keep talking to him, and not only when you are scared, but all the time," he instructed. "He is always there to listen."

Ana smiled her thanks then thought to ask, "How long do you think it will take us to get to Flint Creek where my aunt lives?"

"Well, I have been thinking on it," he began, tilting his head to one side, "and I figure it'll take about two and a half days to reach Austin by train and then about ten hours on to Flint Creek on the stage. Now, that's without any stops, and there will have to be a few stops along the way, so about four or five days maybe."

"Oh my," Ana said, all the while thinking about having to be cooped up on the train for that long.

Ana felt the train begin to slow. Jacob quickly looked out the window and announced that they had made it to Huntsville Depot. He instructed for all of them to wait aboard the train while he went inside. Returning a short time later, he told them he was able to get a quick response to his telegraph.

"Liza, Colonel Lawson wants me to send you on to Texas with the girls as soon as possible. I spoke to the engineer, and they will be ready to head that way in two hours," he informed them.

"What about you?" Ana asked him.

"I'm to head back to Chattanooga in the morning."

Feeling safer with him around, Ana had hoped that he would be able to go with them. She found herself worrying if Mr. Schneider would be able to handle things that might come up.

Seeing the fear creeping up in her face, he was quick to add, "I will stay here with you until the train starts to leave."

"Thank you," she whispered.

"Right now, though, I am going to walk across the street to the mercantile and pick up a few more supplies for the trip."

"Do you need some money? I have what the colonel gave me for the trip," Mr. Schneider offered.

"No, I have plenty for now. He slipped me a few bills before we left too."

With that, Jacob headed for the door. When he came back, he was loaded down with all sorts of food and a few surprises as well.

"I thought you ladies would like to have something to keep you occupied," he said with a big smile on his face. He had bought a small doll for Lucy and a book of Bible stories for Ana.

"Miss Liza, I didn't forget you," he said and handed her a couple of balls of yarn and knitting needles. "I noticed the shawl that you are wearing. I took the chance that you had made it and would know how to use these."

She took the items from Jacob with a hint of tears in her eyes. A quiet, "Thank you'sa" was all she could manage.

"Mr. Schneider, I thought these might come in handy." Jacob handed him a deck of cards and a checker board game. "Maybe you can teach the girls how to play checkers, if they don't already know how."

"I'll do that," Schneider replied.

The next two hours went by a little too fast for Ana, and before she was ready, the train's whistle blew, and Jacob was standing to leave. They all stood with him and began to say their good-byes. Even though they had only known Jacob for a few hours, it somehow seemed much longer. Ana was not sure if she would ever see this man again, but deep down, she sure hoped she would.

"Mr. Schneider, you take good care of these ladies," Jacob said as he and Thomas shook hands.

"Will do, and you take care of yourself, Dalton."

"Miss Liza, it has been a pleasure to meet you. Take care of these girls," Jacob said as he turned her way.

"You know I wills'sa," she responded with confidence.

Jacob offered Liza a smile and turned his attention to Lucy and Ana. "Miss Lucy, you be a good girl now, all right? Take care of everyone for me."

"I will."

"Ana, always remember what I told you." He then pulled her aside for a little privacy. "Talk to Him, all the time. He will make things easier for you."

Ana nodded then asked, "Will we ever see you again, Jacob?"

"Oh, you never know. Once this war is over, I just might have to come for a visit."

She felt he really didn't mean it, but it still felt good to hear him say the words anyway.

"I'll tell you what. For now, you can write to me. How is that? It would be nice to have someone to write to."

"I would like that very much," she answered a little too quickly. "Wait, you don't already have someone to write to, someone who would be upset, maybe, if we wrote to each other?" Ana was too nervous to ask straight out if he had a girlfriend back home.

With a big smile and a wink, signifying his understanding of her meaning, he answered, "Nope."

He gave her a quick hug, turned, waved good-bye to the others, and was out the door. Ana watched him on the platform as the train pulled away, all the while secretly hoping that what he said would come true someday—that she would indeed see him once again.

"I am tired," Lucy whined a short time later.

"It has been a long day," Liza said. "Maybe we should try's and git some sleep somewheres."

"Come, I will show you where you can do just that." Mr. Schneider stood and headed for the rear door.

They all followed him into the next car, which was lined on both sides with bunks.

"You should be able to get a decent night's sleep in here. I will stay in the other car and keep watch." He then tipped his hat and headed for the door.

"Thank you'sa," Liza replied and began readying Lucy for bed.

Ana took care of herself and crawled up into the top berth across from Lucy. Once Liza was finished tucking Lucy in, she turned and did the same for Ana. Even though Ana was getting a little old for tucking, she still liked it.

Standing between them and holding their hands, Liza spoke, "I know this is hard fo' you girls, but we's gonna be jist fine, you will see. Now, let us pray to God an' ask him to be protect'n' us through the night."

Ana and Lucy followed her lead. All the while, Jacob's words were echoing in her mind. *Talk to Him all the time, and He will make things easier.* She made a vow to do that. And in no time after the prayer and after she turned down the lantern, sleep settled in.

4

"WHEN ARE WE going to be there?"

Ana shook her head, for she knew this was the first of many questions from Lucy. Patience had never been one of her strong points.

"Well, it is actually going to be a few days yet before we get to our last stop in Texas," Mr. Schneider began to explain. "But we will have to make a few stops along the way."

"Why?" Lucy wanted to know as she made herself comfortable on the ottoman in front of Thomas's chair.

"To buy supplies and to rest from riding the train."

"Where will we stop?"

Mr. Schneider smiled and gave the girl a pat on her head. "Our first stop will be in Shreveport, Louisiana. We will actually try to get a couple hotel rooms there for the night so we can freshen up a bit." He sat, waiting for the next question that was sure to come.

"When will we be there?"

"We should be there tomorrow, around noon."

"Tomorrow! That's such a long time," she whined in dramatic fashion.

Ana felt the need to rescue the poor man. "Lucy, quit pestering Mr. Schneider. We will get there when we get there. Here, play with the doll Jacob gave you for a while," she suggested as she led her sister over to the sofa. She then placed the doll in Lucy's lap.

Lucy did as she was told but stuck out her lip in protest. She was asking Liza, not long after, if she could go and lie down for a nap.

"My doll is sleepy," Lucy said, rubbing her eyes and finishing with a large yawn.

"Yo' doll, huh? All right, I's be thinkin a nap would be a good idea," Liza said and began ushering her toward the sleeper car.

Ana spent the rest of the afternoon reading the Bible storybook Jacob had given her. Page after page of unbelievable and amazing stories came to life before her eyes. Some she remembered from years past, but many were brand-new to her. The more Ana read, the more she wanted to read. Liza was telling her it was time for supper before she knew it.

Afterward, Mr. Schneider asked Ana and a bored Lucy if they wanted to learn to play checkers. They played on for several hours. They even talked Liza into joining in.

With their thoughts occupied by the game, it took a while to notice Lucy had become very quiet. They looked and found her sound asleep sitting up in her chair. Liza scooped up the sleeping child and headed for bed while Ana helped Mr. Schneider clean up.

Liza had already lain down by the time Ana made it to the bunk car, so Ana did her best to say her prayers all by herself. She was determined to talk to God as much as she could.

They arrived in Shreveport about lunchtime the following day, just as Mr. Schneider promised. Ana began to take in as much of the town as she could while they waited for their things to be unloaded. She was surprised that for such a large town, it was fairly quiet. She only saw a couple of men walking on the boardwalk. Ana decided most everyone must be taking their noontime meal. She felt sure the activity would pick up soon.

They headed across the street to the hotel after securing their belongings. Ana could not wait! It felt as though coal dust covered every inch of her body. Therefore, the first thing she planned to do was bathe.

"I am sure you ladies would like to freshen up and then take it easy for the rest of the afternoon. If you would like, I will head downstairs and have someone send up a bath and a little lunch for you," he offered.

"That would be wonderful'sa," Liza said, adding a grateful smile.

"Thank you, Mr. Schneider," Ana told him as he turned to make his leave.

In no time, they all had a bath, and their stomachs were full. They spent the rest of the afternoon browsing the various shops along the boardwalk and enjoying the bright, sunny summer day.

They took their time in each shop, especially in the mercantile. They had the biggest selection that Ana had ever seen. She could have stayed in there all day. But they had promised Mr. Schneider they would meet him in the hotel for supper, and it was nearing that time.

Ana had the sensation that someone was following them as they made their way toward the hotel. She looked around and noticed a small group of men but decided to ignore them.

Once they arrived at the restaurant, they found Mr. Schneider waiting. He led them to a table, where they sat and began to look over the menu.

After a few minutes, Ana realized the men who had been following them had entered the restaurant as well and were watching their every move from a table nearby. Mr. Schneider noticed them too and tried to start a conversation with them.

"Good evening, gentlemen. Nice evening out."

"Um-hum," was the only offered response.

Ana began to study the group. There were four total, and not one of them appeared to be of decent character. She watched as one in particular pierced Liza with dark, evil eyes. Fear began to rise within her, and she found herself wishing the men would decide to leave. The one watching Liza finally took his gaze from her and spoke.

"Well, lookie here, boys," he began. "Looks like we got us an educated slave."

"Is she really readin' that thing, or is she just pretendin'?" another wanted to know as he stood and headed toward them.

Liza gently folded the menu and placed it on the table, keeping her eyes low. She had always been strong and confident, but Ana watched all of that slip away.

"Now, gentlemen, we don't want any trouble," Mr. Schneider said as he started to stand.

"Trouble?" The evil eyed man scoffed. "Trouble is slaves that can read and think they can waltz around our town as they please."

"Now, sir, let's not do this. We are only passing through, and we will be out of here in the morning."

"I think you need to get out of town now and take that piece of trash with you."

"How dare you dare talk about Liza that way!" Ana screamed, causing the man to come at her. She picked up the nearest thing for defense she could, which happened to be a steak knife. She pointed the weapon at him, daring him to take another step.

"If this don't beat all!" The man stopped his advance and laughed. The rest of the men joined in.

"Ana Grace, sit down!" Liza begged.

"Yeah, little girl, you mind that slave woman of yours."

"She is not a slave! She is a free woman!"

"Ana! Let me handle this!" Mr. Schneider ordered as he made it to her side and took the knife from her trembling hand. He then turned and addressed the other man with amazing calm. "Let us take our food upstairs, and we will leave you gentlemen alone."

"That's a good idea, Jim. Let 'em head on upstairs," one of the other men said in an attempt to calm the escalating situation.

"Get on up there then, and you best be on that train and out of here in the mornin'!"

Mr. Schneider gathered up his plate and drink, and the women followed his lead. They then made their way up the stairs and to their rooms.

"You ladies get in there and lock that door, you hear?" Thomas instructed when they reached their rooms.

"Yes'sa, Mr. Schneider. I'm sho' sorry fo' the trouble'sa." The quiver in her voice made it clear she was still upset by the whole thing.

"No apologies necessary, Miss Liza. They are a bunch of belligerent fools, and we shan't worry about them anymore."

The three headed inside, sat, and began trying to finish their meal. However, all Lucy wanted to do was sit in Liza's lap and hold on for dear life. She soon fell asleep, and after Liza put her to bed, she came to Ana's side.

"Ya' should not a done that, Ana Grace."

Ana knew she was referring to her outburst.

"I couldn't let them talk about you that way, Liza." Tears began to make their way down her cheeks.

"Now, now," Liza said as she wrapped her arms around her. "I am used to people like that. They don't botha' me."

"Yes, they did bother you, Liza, I could tell."

"Well, you can't let it botha' you, sweet girl. It is all ova now. Les try to git some sleep."

Ana decided that was probably for the best and began to ready herself for bed. As nice as it had been to walk around a new town, she could not wait to be on that train in the morning.

5

THEY WERE ON the train and pulling out of Shreveport early the next morning. Although Ana knew each of them had the previous evening on their minds, the trip from the hotel to the depot was uneventful. They each let out a huge sigh of relief as the train reached the city limits, each of them thankful to be back on the rails.

About thirty minutes into the ride, the train came to a screeching halt, sending the lot of them tumbling to the floor. Lucy began to cry, and Ana and Liza rushed to her side. Mr. Schneider went to see what was going on and was no sooner out the door when he was coming back in, ushered by the barrel of a shotgun.

"Now, git over there with the womenfolk and don't be tryin' nothin' stupid," the man with the gun ordered.

Ana took a good look at him, and terror washed over her as she realized he was one of the men from the night before.

The three ladies took a seat on the couch. Mr. Schneider stood between them and the intruder.

"What is going on here?" Mr. Schneider demanded to know.

"Once my boss gits in here, he'll tell ya'," he finished with a spit to the floor, all the while maintaining his aim.

A few minutes later, the evil-eyed man, the one they called Jim, came through the door. He stood before them with a devilish smile curling the corners of his mouth, never taking his eyes off Liza. She kept her head low and tried her best to comfort a frightened Lucy.

"What's this all about?" Mr. Schneider tried again to get some answers.

"This is about that piece of trash, right there," Jim said, pointing a dirty finger at the frightened woman.

"I don't understand."

"Let me explain it to ya' then," he growled through clenched teeth as he walked up to Mr. Schneider. With his face mere inches from Mr. Schneider's, he continued, "I have a real problem with the likes of her. Walking around, acting as if she's as good as me.

"She should be on some plantation somewhere working her fingers to the bone so the massa can reap the benefits. Staying put in her little shack at night until the massa decides he wants a little of what she has to offer." He offered a knowing grin. "I'm thinking that we're gonna take that trash off your hands and take her and show her how a good little slave is supposed to act." He then reached around Thomas and grabbed Liza by the arm, jerking her to her feet.

Ana could stay quiet no longer. She jumped to her feet and began to attack the beast.

"You are not taking her anywhere, you filthy monster!" She pounded her fists into his chest with all she had.

The last thing Ana remembered before Jim sent her flying through the air was the ear-piercing screams of a terrified Lucy.

Ana awoke on the chaise with a thunderous pain in her head. She realized the sun was beginning to fade as she slowly opened her eyes. She tried to recall when and why she had lain down, but for the life of her, she couldn't remember. She could see Lucy and Mr. Schneider sitting at the dining table, engrossed in a game of checkers as she forced her pounding head off the soft cushions of the lounger.

Mr. Schneider had his back to her, but she could see by Lucy's face that she had been crying. Ana figured she had probably gotten upset because Mr. Schneider refused to let her cheat. She then looked around for Liza and decided she had probably gone to the necessary. Standing on wobbly legs, she made her way toward the game of checkers.

The two players looked up as soon as she reached the side of the table. Lucy began to cry, and Ana looked to Mr. Schneider and saw a nasty cut on his cheek and a bruise encircling one of his eyes. She took a closer look and discovered his mouth and nose had been bleeding as well.

The sight of him caused the memory of what had happened to come flooding back, and Ana felt her knees buckle beneath her. Mr. Schneider quickly came to her rescue, catching her before she hit the floor, and then helped her back to the chaise. Once seated, Lucy crawled up beside her and held on for dear life.

"How are you feeling, Miss Ana? You took a pretty good lick to the back of your head. Luckily, the skin wasn't broken, but you have a nice lump back there."

Ana reached up to feel for herself, causing pain to shoot through her entire head. "Where is Liza? I think I need some tonic."

Lucy squeezed her tighter. When no one answered, she looked up to find Mr. Schneider with tear-filled eyes.

"Mr. Schneider, where is she?" Her heart began to pound out of her chest.

"They took her, Miss Ana," he choked out. "I tried to stop them, but there were too many."

"Then we will go back and get her," she said matter-of-factly. "We will go to Shreveport, tell the sheriff what happened, and we will get her back."

"No, Miss Ana, we can't." He began to cry.

"Why not?"

"They…," he began, looking reluctantly at Lucy. Ana could tell he didn't want to talk in front of her.

"Lucy, go climb up on your bunk, and I will come in and read you a story in a few minutes, all right?"

"I don't want to leave you, Ana!"

"I promise I will be in there soon."

Lucy looked at her with uncertainty but slowly released her hold and began to make her way to the bunk car. The fear inside Ana began to well up as she watched her sister walk away. *What could be so bad that he didn't want to discuss it in front of Lucy?*

She looked to Mr. Schneider and willed him to continue as soon as Lucy disappeared into the next car.

"She is gone, Miss Ana."

"Gone?" Ana's breath caught in her throat. "What do you mean *gone*, Mr. Schneider?"

"They hung her." His voice was a gravelly whisper.

"What? No...no, you are mistaken. They only pretended...to scare us! They wouldn't be that cruel!"

After a moment of trying to process this new information, a terrible thought came to mind.

"Did Lucy see this?" Ana asked, trying to maintain control of her emotions.

"No, she did not. They bound her hands and feet and put her in the sleeper car. I freed her as soon as I could. They messed up the engineer and the rest of the crew pretty good too."

"Should they be driving the train?"

"They said they were all right. The schedule has us stopping in Marshall, Texas, but I told them to keep going on to Tyler instead. We should be there anytime."

"We can't pretend this didn't happen. We have to do something." Ana allowed her emotions to break free. "Liza was like a grandmother to us!" She covered her face with her hands as a torrent of sobs tore through her body.

"I know, sweetie. I know." Thomas did his best to comfort her. "I have plans to go straight to the sheriff's office when we get to town. I will tell them everything, from the restaurant last night to what happened today. I will give the names of the men I remember too."

"Jim...the main one...the one with the scary eyes...they called him Jim."`

"Yes, I remember. They will pay for this, I promise. Maybe not here on earth, but God will make sure they pay."

"You really believe there's a God after this? I was beginning to believe in all of that myself. But Papa was right after all. There's no God! If there was, He wouldn't have taken my mama and my dear sweet Liza."

"You don't mean that—," he tried, but she cut him short.

"Yes, I do. There will be no more talk of God around my sister and me. Do you understand?"

"I understand, Miss Ana." Thomas dropped his head in defeat.

Ana stood and made her way to the sleepers to tend to her baby sister, wiping the tears from her face as she went. She climbed into Lucy's bunk and sat holding the child, the promise of a story forgotten. A short time later, the train began to slow, and Ana made her way to a window where she could see the outline of the town ahead.

Ana spent one of the longest nights of her life in that town. She lay awake, letting her mind wander over the worst heartaches in her life. First, her mother died and left her and her little sister with a father who, at the first sign of trouble, sent them away to an aunt whom they had never even met. Then someone took their dear Liza away from them! Was she really supposed to trust in a God who let it all happen?

Ana realized they would have to go ahead to Aunt Josie's, but she planned on having a long talk with her father as soon as they were back in Chattanooga. He was going to learn exactly how she felt about him always being gone.

She convinced herself he would quit the army and, for once in their lives, devote all his time to their being a family. She fell asleep that night snuggled up to Lucy, with plans for the future rolling through her mind.

The train pulled out of Tyler about four o'clock the next afternoon, and Mr. Schneider informed them their next stop would be in Hempstead. However, since it would be late at night, they would not leave the train. The crew would secure supplies they were not able to find in Tyler, and then they would head back out.

The evening was a boring one for sure. All Lucy wanted to do was sleep or sit snuggled up as close to her big sister as she could get. She did take comfort in the doll that Jacob had given her, though. Ana teased her that if she squeezed it any tighter, it would start crying. Lucy smiled a little, but increased her hold on the toy.

Mr. Schneider acted all day as though he was afraid to speak to either of them. He spent his time playing cards by himself or staring out the window, breaking long enough to make sure the girls had their meals, and then he would be back to his business. That night, around nine o'clock, Lucy began to complain about being tired.

"I will help you get ready for bed and tuck you in." Ana stood and headed for the sleepers.

"I want Mr. Schneider to tuck me in."

Mr. Schneider looked to Ana in surprise but nodded and rose from the table and headed their way. Ana readied Lucy, and then Mr. Schneider lifted her up into her bunk, pulled the covers up tight, and gave her a tender smile.

"Thank you, Mr. Schneider," Lucy said in a sleepy voice.

"You are quite welcome, little lady," he said and then turned to leave.

"Mr. Schneider?"

"Yes, Lucy?"

"Can I call you Thomas?"

"It is, *may I*," Ana corrected. "Besides, being so forward is rude behavior. He would have told us by now if he wanted to be called Thomas."

"No…no, Miss Ana," he began while waving his hand in the air. "It's quite all right. I would be very happy if you both called me Thomas from now on."

"Good," Lucy announced. "I like the name *Thomas*."

"I am glad you do. And I absolutely love the name *Lucy*." He then looked at Ana and offered a smile. "You two girls have a good night's sleep. Remember, we will be stopping soon, so don't let it frighten you."

Ana suddenly felt ashamed at the way she had treated him earlier, and tears began to fill her eyes.

"I'm sorry, Mr. Schneider, for the way I acted before."

"Shh…," he began as he made his way over to her and put his hands on her shoulders. "It's all right, child. Everything is going to be all right. I realize all of this has been hard on you, so no hard feelings." He finished with a quick hug and a kiss to her cheek. "Get some sleep now."

"All right," Ana answered as she wiped at her tears.

"And please, do call me Thomas," he added when he reached the door.

6

August 26, 1863

ANA AWOKE THE next morning as the train was beginning to slow. In her sleepy state, she figured they were pulling into Hempstead. She opened her eyes, pulled back the curtain on her bunk, and discovered the sun was already up. She realized she had slept straight through the train stopping during the night, and now they were in Austin. She marveled at how far they had come as she pulled herself up in the bunk.

Her sister's giggles drifted through the sleeper car as the train grew quiet. Then, from out of nowhere, she thought she heard the familiar voice of her dear Liza. The reality of the past few days came crashing down hard on top of her.

Ana lay back in her bunk and cried until there were simply no more tears left to cry. Slowly, a peaceful calm washed over her, and it seemed as if she could feel Liza's gentle touch on her head.

She then began to hear the soft words of comfort Liza had often used. *Now, now, lil' one. Everythin's gonna be all right. You see.* For the first time in what seemed like a lifetime, Ana believed that it actually would.

Ana found renewed strength and climbed out of bed, dried her eyes, and readied herself for the day. Thomas had informed them the day before that they would probably be in Austin for a couple of days. He was unaware of the schedule of the local stage and knew that most places didn't have regular service. Therefore, with the possibility of an extended stay, Ana determined herself to have a great time in this new town.

Peering out the window at the city sights, Ana could see this town was indeed one in which to have an adventure. Buildings stretched up and down both sides of a wide dirt street. She had difficulty seeing exactly what the buildings were because of the location of the depot. But from her vantage point, Ana could see many shops to explore during their time here.

Wagons of all sizes and styles, along with riders on horseback, were traveling the street. A steady flow of people were making their way around the spacious boardwalks lined up in front of the buildings. Ana was pleased to see that not one woman appeared to be wearing hoops under their skirts. She realized that was the fashion of the times but so hated their cumbersomeness and looked forward to the freedom of not having to wear one.

A sense of excitement bubbled up inside her, and for the first time in what seemed like forever, Ana actually looked forward to what lay ahead. Suddenly, Lucy came running into the sleeper car, and Ana could tell by the gleam in her eyes that she was excited as well.

"Thomas wanted me to come wake you up so we could go into town for breakfast, but you are already up!" All her words ran together in her excitement, causing Ana to laugh.

"Yes, I am. I was looking out at the town. It's pretty remarkable, is it not?"

"Yes, can we go now?" Lucy grabbed her sister by the hand and started dragging her toward the door.

"Yes, we can go! Leave the arm attached, though, if you don't mind!"

Ana and Lucy shared a laugh as they made their way through the cars. Before they knew it, they were off the train and waiting on the platform for Thomas. He had gone inside the station to send off a telegram to their father and to inquire about the stage.

He informed them when he returned from inside that a stage that would be able to take them to Flint Creek was due the next morning. The girls were excited to learn they would have all day to explore this new town. He paid someone to take their things to the hotel and then began leading the way down the boardwalk.

Ana took in as much of her surroundings as she possibly could. They walked past Levi and Phelps, a dry goods store. Across the street, Ana could see Thompson's Millinery, with a multitude of beautiful hats decorating the window. Next door to the millinery was a lovely-looking fabric shop by the name of Rose's. Thomas noticed Ana's interest in these two shops and promised to take her there later.

On down the boardwalk was an apothecary, a candle store, and the Austin Hotel with an actual theater attached. They walked right past Bell's Saloon. Piano music spilled into the outside air from inside, along with the scent of tobacco, dirty men, and cheap perfume. Ana caught a quick peek inside as one of the patrons exited and was surprised and appalled at the sight therein.

Women with their chests half exposed were sitting on the men's laps! The men were laughing and putting their hands on the women as if they were nothing but a piece of meat! Thomas grabbed her arm before she could react and escorted both girls away as fast as he could. Once they were well away from the boisterous place, Ana stopped and looked up at him.

"Why would those women let the men touch them like that?"

"Well…" He cleared his throat and continued dryly, "They're not very decent women. I don't want either of you to go near that place again. You wouldn't have gone that close this time, if I had been paying attention. From now on, we will cross the street to go past."

Ana nodded, turned, and continued to walk, trying all the while to push the images from the saloon out of her mind.

They were in the restaurant a few minutes later. They followed the waiter to a table in the back of the room. Once seated, they began looking over the menu. Ana had to shake from her mind the memories of the last time they were in a restaurant together.

She determined to have a good time and forced herself to ignore the pain in her heart. Soon they were feasting on a bountiful meal of mouthwatering biscuits and gravy with all the trimmings. Stomachs full, Thomas announced he was ready to make good on his promise and escorted them toward the hat shop.

"Oooh, I like this one, Ana!" Lucy exclaimed, holding her find up for her sister to see.

It was a green felt toque and had a nest of brown feathers on top, with an ugly stuffed bird in it. It really was a hideous thing, and Ana had to fight the urge to make a face.

"Yes, Lucy, that is nice." Ana then spied the bonnets. "I wonder if Aunt Josie wears bonnets." Ana directed this to Thomas, who was standing in the corner of the room, hands stuffed in his pockets, looking rather uncomfortable with his surroundings.

"I wouldn't know. Why?"

"I thought if we had the money, I could get her a gift. You know, to thank her for letting Lucy and me come and stay."

"A gift is a wonderful idea, but let me make a suggestion. Since this is the first store we have gone in and there is so much more to see in this town, why not pick out a bonnet and commit it to memory. At the end of the day, if you have not found anything else you like better, you can come back and get it."

"That is a grand idea, Thomas, thank you."

"You are quite welcome."

They stayed in there for a few more minutes and then made their way down the street, stopping in almost every store. Ana ended up finding something in each store she would like to get for Aunt Josie, so before long, her head was spinning with the possibilities. Choosing was shaping up to be a difficult task.

They made their way into the small building housing the candle shop around lunchtime. To their surprise, there was a counter inside where they served soup. They decided to have lunch first and then browse the merchandise once their stomachs were full again.

Ana began to look around at the various items in the shop as she ate. There were candles of all shapes, sizes, and colors. She had rarely ever seen colored candles, so those quickly became her favorites.

The shop also carried all sorts of candle holders. A large selection of brass holders of many shapes and sizes covered one table. Another was loaded with hand-carved wooden ones and one with shiny silver ones. The collection that intrigued Ana the most, however, was the one located on a shelf up against the back wall.

She had never seen such delicate pieces in all her life and could hardly eat from staring at the beautiful, glistening glass. She headed over to them as soon as her last bite was down. Ana knew the gift she was searching for could be in that collection. Still, after searching for a few minutes, she was not able to find anything close to perfect.

She overheard the shop owner explaining to Thomas that all the glass pieces were handblown. Ana was intrigued and began to inquire about the process.

The man started to explain but stopped midsentence. "How about you all follow me out back for a little demonstration?"

"Can we, Thomas?" Lucy asked, jumping up and down.

"Yes, Thomas, please?" Ana added.

"Sure, sounds like fun," Thomas agreed.

They followed the man out the back of the store to his workshop. He pointed out a big oven he called a *kiln*. He picked up a long iron rod that had been propped against the kiln and some big iron tongs. He then retrieved a red-hot glowing wad of what he said was melted glass from the kiln with the tongs and placed it on the end of the rod. He placed the end of the rod with the glass on it back in the kiln. They watched as the glass began to get even hotter, causing it to melt more and surround the end of the rod.

Next he pulled the rod from the fire and began to blow into the end of the rod where he was holding it, making the glass bubble up on the other end. He took a red dye and streaked the glass with it, and then taking a piece of smooth iron about the size of a small kitchen knife, he began to shape the glass. As he used the piece of iron to smooth the glass, he turned the rod in the opposite direction, creating a gentle swirl in the glass, the streaks of red creating a very elegant effect.

He would place the glass back in the fire occasionally to keep it good and hot and then go back to shaping it. He finished by forming the base; and then with a gentle clip, with a tool that looked like a giant pair of scissors, he disconnected the piece from the rod.

"That was wonderful! Thank you so much for showing us!" Ana was so impressed with the whole thing. She felt as though she could sit and watch him for hours.

"You're welcome."

"The way you used the red dye made it the most exquisite thing I have ever seen!"

"Well, if you would rather have this piece instead of one from inside, you can."

"I can do that…really?" Ana then turned to Thomas. "Is that all right, Thomas?"

"Well, if that is the one you want, then we shall get it," Thomas told her.

"Thank you, Thomas!"

This brought a protest from Lucy. "I want to get Aunt Josie something too!"

Ana went to her with a suggestion. "I have an idea, Lucy. I saw some beautiful red candles in the shop that would go great with the glass holder. You should pick out one of those for Aunt Josie." Ana suddenly realized she probably should have ran the idea past Thomas first, so she looked his way, and he nodded his approval.

"I could do that," Lucy said with pleasure.

The owner wrapped the piece in a cloth to protect it, and they headed back inside to let Lucy pick out the candle. She headed straight for the boxes of red-colored ones and began her search. She settled on a long tapered style, which had tiny carved flowers in it. The carvings went down into the wax past the red and into the white, creating a wonderful contrast in the colors. It was perfect!

The shop owner's wife took both pieces and placed them in a wooden box full of straw for protection. She then wrapped the box in beautiful pink cloth, finishing the presentation with a big white bow. Lucy and Ana were thrilled! They left the store with their treasure and headed toward the hotel.

Lucy and Ana finished the day with a long, hot bath, letting it melt away the tiredness they each felt from the long train ride and a day of shopping. It was time for dinner by the time they were dressed and their hair combed and dried some, so they headed to the top of the stairs to wait for Thomas as they had promised. He was already there waiting for them.

"I was beginning to think I was going to have to send someone in there to check to see if you had drowned."

"Oh, Thomas," Lucy laughed, "you are so funny!"

Thomas and Ana shared in the laughter as they headed down the stairs to dinner.

"I assume you ladies had a nice bath?"

"Yes, it was very nice. Thank you for ordering it for us," Ana told him.

"I had to," he said and then wrinkled up his nose. "You two were beginning to smell!" He finished with a wave of his hand in front of his nose.

"That's not very nice!" Ana protested through laughter.

"I didn't smell!" Lucy argued. "I really don't now. The nice lady put rose oil in the water." Lucy took a big sniff of her arm to emphasize her point.

Ana began to think about the day as she and Lucy lay in bed later that night. It truly was one of the best days ever. She was glad she had apologized to Thomas. He was a very good and kindhearted man, and she was beginning to think fondly of him.

As sleep began to claim her, Ana suddenly felt as though she could hear Liza praying. Then the words that Jacob spoke to her before he left came to mind. *Talk to Him. He will make things easier.* Ana quickly pushed those thoughts from her head and demanded sleep to come. She just wasn't ready to forgive God yet.

7

ANA AND LUCY woke later than usual the next morning. It was a beautiful sunny day out, and they were excited about their upcoming trip by stagecoach. They dressed and headed for the door, but as they neared it, they saw a note lying on the floor. Ana picked it up and read aloud:

> I hope you slept well. I decided to allow you to sleep late since yesterday was such a tiresome day. Check to see if I am in my room once you have dressed. If I am not, head downstairs to the dining room and choose whatever you would like to eat.
>
> I am heading to the telegraph office to check for a response from your father. I will be back soon.
>
> Don't forget. The stage leaves at 11:00 a.m. sharp!
>
> Thomas

"I hope we can hear from Papa," Lucy said wistfully.

"I do too. I miss him terribly."

"I wonder if he knows about Liza yet."

"He does if he has gotten any of Thomas's telegrams."

"I miss Liza." Tears filled Lucy's eyes. Ana wrapped her arms around her sister and held on tight.

They headed toward Thomas's room a few minutes later and found him gone. They did as Thomas had instructed and headed downstairs to breakfast. They hadn't been eating long when Thomas made his way into the dining room.

"Good morning. I see you found my note," he said as he took a seat.

"Yes. Did we get word from Papa?" Ana asked, getting straight to the point.

Thomas looked at both of them and nodded as he pulled the telegram from his pocket and began to read,

> UPSET TO LEARN OF LIZA—*stop*—WILL BE IN TOUCH WITH AUTHORITIES IN SHREVEPORT AS SOON AS POSSIBLE—*stop*—FIGHTING SPORADIC HERE—*stop*—HOME DESTROYED—*stop*—GIVE MY LOVE TO GIRLS—*stop*—INFORM ME OF ARRIVAL IN FLINT CREEK—*stop*
>
> LT COLONEL JAMES LAWSON

"What does de-stroy-ed mean?" Lucy wanted to know as soon as he was finished reading.

"It means our house was torn up." Ana began to cry. It slowly sank in for Lucy, and she began to cry as well.

"I know this is hard news to hear, girls," Thomas began. "But the most important thing was spared."

Both gave him questioning looks.

"Your father."

"That is true," Ana said and began to dry her tears. "That is what is most important, Lucy."

"But I love our house."

"So do I, but with the shelling going on when we left, we should have known something like this could happen."

Lucy nodded then looked to Thomas with wide eyes. "They blew up the store next to the church! I saw it!"

"I saw it too," he told her. "Let us think on better things from this point on. We have a big day ahead of us, and we only have an hour to finish getting things ready."

Ana and Lucy agreed and made quick work of the rest of their breakfast. Afterward, they headed up to gather their things. Thomas stayed behind to secure a box of food for the trip and, when he finished, made his way upstairs to make sure the girls were ready to go. In no time, the three of them sat on the front porch of the hotel, surrounded by their trunks and satchels, waiting for their trip to continue.

They watched as the stage turned the corner at the end of the street and began heading their way. Each of them stood and made their way to the edge of the platform, watching as the team came to a halt and the men jumped from the top to begin loading their things.

"Mr. Schneider, Mr. Schneider!"

Ana looked to see a small-framed man wearing glasses and a dark-green visor running their way, waving a piece of paper over his head.

"It's the gentleman from the telegraph desk," Thomas informed them as the man made his way onto the porch.

"Mr. Schneider…you have received…another telegram," he said in a winded voice as he handed Thomas the note. "I am glad I was…able to catch you."

"Yes, as am I. Thank you, sir," Thomas told the man as he took the note.

The man nodded at the girls and then turned back to Thomas. "Would you like me to wait while you read it, in case you need to reply?" he asked, finally in control of his breathing.

"Yes, yes, of course," Thomas answered and then began to unfold the telegram. Ana and Lucy moved closer and waited for him to begin.

> SENDING SGT DALTON TO SHREVEPORT TO HELP AUTHORITIES—*stop*—WILL NO-TIFY YOU OF PROGRESS—*stop*
>
> LT COLONEL JAMES LAWSON

"Do you need to reply, sir?"

"No, no reply needed," Thomas told the man and then reached to shake his hand. "Thank you, sir."

"My pleasure. You have a nice trip now." He then turned and headed back off the porch and down the street.

Thomas helped Ana and her sister board the coach and then signaled to the driver that they were ready. With a quick lunge forward, they began to roll toward their final destination.

Ana watched as the town shrank in the distance and then turned her attention to the view that lay ahead. She kept telling herself that things were going to work out fine. Jacob was going to find the men who hurt Liza and help bring them to justice. The war would soon end, and then they would make their way back home to their father.

It didn't take long for the thrill of being on the stage to fade away. The ride was rough, hot, and dusty, and Lucy grew more and more ill by the minute. She was constantly complaining about it being too hot or too bouncy, or she was hungry or tired. Each complaint from her contained more drama than the last.

Ana was on the verge of giving in to the urge to toss her out the door when they came to a stop. The driver hopped down and announced they were going to take lunch and give the horses a break since they had just come through some rough terrain. Ana stepped out of the coach, stretched her arms and legs, and began to take in her surroundings.

It was actually a lovely spot. There were many shade trees and there was a small creek running down along the side of the trail. She picked a spot under a huge oak tree close to the creek and began to set out their picnic, that Thomas had gotten for them.

It did them all good to be out of the stage for a while. They ate their meal and then allowed Lucy to run and play as much as she wanted. Ana was secretly hoping to tire her out. She even gave in and let her sister take off her shoes and wade in the creek.

Ana began to wonder about their chaperone once they were back on the trail. He had sort of fallen into their lives, but in the very short time they had known him, he had become very important to her and to Lucy as well. Ana realized she knew absolutely nothing about him and decided to remedy that.

"Thomas, I've been thinking."

"Um, what on?" he said, turning his attention her way.

"Well…I realized I don't really know anything about you."

"What would you like to know?"

"For starters, where exactly are you from? I don't recall ever having seen you around Chattanooga before."

"I actually came to Chattanooga about five years ago. I was living in a small town in Alabama and came north to find work." He paused.

"Go on," Ana coaxed, her curiosity causing Thomas to grin.

"All right, here goes." He then began to paint Ana a picture of his life. "Like I said, I'm originally from Alabama. It was a very small rural area, populated by nothing but small farmers and sharecroppers. My wife, Nancy, and I grew up there together." His expression turned sad for a moment.

"Anyways…I helped sharecrop with my father until about seven years ago when my wife took ill with consumption. I started staying home to take care of her. She passed about nine months into her illness.

"By this time, my father's health was deteriorating, and he had given up farming. Since I didn't have a job and jobs were hard to come by at home, and since my parents needed help to make ends meet, I headed north to Chattanooga and was blessed to find this job."

"As a conductor?"

"Yes."

Ana could see by the distant look in his eyes that the memories were getting to him. "I'm so sorry about your wife, Thomas. I know it has to be really hard on you."

"At times, it is."

"What about your parents?"

"They have both passed on now."

"I'm so sorry."

"I miss all of them terribly."

"I know what you mean. It hurts my heart so much when I think about Mama and now Liza."

"I know it does. Never stop thinking about them, though. Always keep them alive in your heart. And make sure that little one does the same." He pointed to a sleeping Lucy.

"I will. I worry about that sometimes. She was so young when Mama passed. She already doesn't remember anything about her."

"That's where you come in. Make sure you tell her every story about your mama you can think of."

"I will try," she told him, needing to change the subject to keep from crying. "I guess that's why I never saw you around town, because you were always on the train."

"I guess so."

"Will you head back to Chattanooga once you deliver us to Aunt Josie?"

"I don't know. I've been thinking on that a lot since we set out, and I think I've decided to wait and see what this new town has to offer me."

"You would really consider staying on in Texas?" Ana was surprised.

"I'm not getting any younger, so why not? I think a change would do me some good."

"I would love it if you would stay. I am actually rather nervous about this whole thing, so it would do wonders for me and Lucy to have a familiar face around."

"Then it's settled! I will stay. At least until you two girls get settled."

"Great! This trip might not be so bad after all."

"Of course not! Think about it as a learning adventure. There is always room for more learning, and how better to learn than to live?"

Ana smiled and nodded her agreement. She then turned her attention to the horizon, the sun having almost faded. She found herself hoping that the lessons were not to be harder ones as she gazed at the purples and pinks painted before her. She felt as though she had learned enough of those to last a lifetime.

The driver pulled the stage into a treelined area to make camp just before the light in the sky was completely gone for the day. He and his partner started a fire and got ready to bed down for the night.

"Thomas, what are we going to do?"

"I will sleep outside with the drivers, and of course, you girls will stay in here," he instructed a worried Ana.

"It's kind of scary being out in the middle of nowhere."

"We will all be fine, I promise. I will sleep as close to the coach as I can, if that will help ease your fears."

"Yes, I believe it would. Thank you, Thomas."

"It's my pleasure. Now, get a good night's sleep. You have a big day tomorrow." With that, he was out the door.

Ana did what she could to get Lucy and herself in a comfortable position and then tried to fall asleep. As it turned out, it was a more difficult task than she had hoped.

8

August 28, 1863

THEY SET OUT the next morning not long after sunup. The driver informed them they had only a couple of hours to go on their journey, and Ana could not wait until it was over. She had decided not long into this part of the trip that she never wanted to ride another stagecoach again. A few more hours, and it would all be over, at least until they headed back home.

Lucy's attitude made it clear she hated the stage more than everyone else put together. Therefore, Ana did her best to keep her sister occupied with games. They played "I'm thinking of something" and "Cupid's coming," and she read to her from the Bible storybook. The diversion worked, and before Ana knew it, Thomas was pointing out the window at the town ahead. Finally they had made it!

They pulled into Flint Creek about nine o'clock in the morning and headed straight for the stagecoach office.

Ana spotted her as soon as they pulled up to the platform in front of an aging log building. She felt the breath rush from her body as she stared straight into the eyes of a woman who could have been her mother's twin. Since Ana looked a lot like her mother herself, it was as if she was looking into a mirror and seeing a glimpse of the future.

Her dark-green eyes sparkled in the morning light. Dark hair, pulled on top of her head, had evidence of curls, like Ana's and her mother's, escaping and dancing in the breeze. Ana knew she ran a ranch, and she decided her attire was probably appropriate for such a life. It would just take some time getting used to seeing a woman dressed in breeches.

The door to the coach opened, and Thomas escorted a still-dazed Ana out onto the platform. She snapped out of it long enough to collect her sister and then headed toward the woman waiting for them.

Josie stood with her hand over her mouth as though she was trying to keep from crying. She spoke as soon as Ana and Lucy stopped in front of her. "I am so glad you are finally here!"

Josie then wrapped her arms around the girls. All the worries Ana had about meeting this woman faded instantly away.

They finished their embrace, and Josie stood looking at her nieces. Finally, she turned to Lucy. "You are so pretty! You look so much like your father."

Lucy smiled with pleasure over this, and then Josie turned to Ana. "And you," she began, "are the spitting image of your mother."

"I was going to say the same thing about you," Ana told her, causing them both to laugh.

Josie's countenance grew serious as the laughter faded. "I'm so sorry about Liza. It had to be a horrible ordeal for the two of you. It breaks my heart your father or I was not there for you."

"How did you know?"

"I received a telegram."

Ana looked to Thomas, and he smiled.

"It *was* hard. We are trying to move past it, as Liza would have wanted. Besides, we weren't alone." Ana smiled with appreciation at Thomas.

"Who is this distinguished-looking gentleman you have with you anyway?" Josie asked.

"Aunt Josie," Ana began the introduction, "this is Thomas Schneider. He works for the railroad, and Papa hired him to bring us to you."

"And we've decided to keep him!" Lucy announced, and laughter filled the air.

"It is a pleasure to meet you, ma'am," Thomas finally was able to say and finished with a tip of his hat.

"It's a pleasure to meet you too. I bet all of you would appreciate a hot meal about now. My wagon is right around the corner. We will get all your things loaded and head on out to my place."

"Uh, ma'am, could you direct me to a hotel or boarding house in town?" Thomas asked Josie.

"Whatever for?"

"Well," he began, "I figured I would go ahead and get settled myself."

"That's a good idea. But you can do it at my place," she told him.

Thomas opened his mouth to protest, but Josie stopped him short with a wave of her hand. "I have plenty of room, and I won't take no for an answer. Besides, it is the least I can do after you took time out of your life to bring my nieces all this way. Most of all, for helping them get through the events of the past few days."

Thomas stood, clearly uncomfortable with the idea.

"You can stay in my guesthouse, if it will make you feel better," she said, trying to convince him.

"You have two houses?" Lucy asked in amazement.

"It is actually the house I started out in here. I built a new and bigger house on my property as my ranching business grew. I keep the old house up for moments like this."

"I think it would be perfect!" Ana said, looking at Thomas and hoping he would agree.

"I guess I could do that, if you're sure you don't mind," he said to Josie.

"I'm the one that offered, so of course, I don't mind," she ended her matter-of-fact statement with a teasing smile. "It's settled then. Let's get your things to the wagon."

They paused long enough for Thomas to head into the telegraph office to get a message off to the girls' father, and then they were on their way.

The wagon ride to the ranch felt like it took no time at all. Ana spent the ride taking in as much of the beautiful territory as possible. Josie told them they referred to this part of Texas as Hill Country. One could definitely see why.

There were mountains and hills where Ana came from. However, these hills seem to roll gently along, one right after another. The trees still were heavy with their summer foliage. Wildflowers of every color were scattered everywhere. In addition, a gentle flowing creek wound its way through it all.

They soon rounded a bend, and the most wonderful sight appeared! A field of delicate purple flowers stretched as far as the eye could see. Josie noticed Ana's excitement and informed her they were lavender.

Josie motioned for her to sniff the air. Ana did and, in doing so, was overtaken by the most wonderful and intoxicating scent. She pondered where she had smelled these flowers before. She noticed Josie watching her.

"Something familiar?" Josie asked with a knowing smile on her face.

"Yes, it is." Then, from out of nowhere, a memory from Ana's past came drifting into her mind.

"*Mother*—she wore a perfume that smelled like this!"

Ana looked to Josie. Neither spoke a word, just shared a smile and the sweet memory of her mother. Josie then turned her focus back to the road ahead and left Ana to her thoughts.

The jerking of the wagon brought Ana back to reality, and she looked to find they were heading through a large wooden gate. Two massive wooden posts stood on either side, with a wrought iron arch stretching across to connect the two. From the middle of the arch hung a wrought iron *K*, which Ana knew stood for *Keller*, Josie's last name. Large corrals lined both sides of the road and held some of the prettiest horses she had ever seen.

Ana marveled at how graceful the animals appeared. She could almost see herself astride one of them, like a real cowgirl, riding across the lavender fields as fast as the horse would take her.

She turned her attention to a couple of black-and-white Border collies as they came running out of a massive two-story barn and up to the wagon barking their greetings. Each fought to be in the lead as they escorted the wagon right up to the front of the house.

Gray rock lined the first story of the large home while the second story boasted gray weathered wood siding. An expansive covered porch stretched across the entire front of the house. Cane-bottom rocking chairs lined the porch, and large wooden swings hung at each end. Two large oak trees, one of which had another swing hanging from it, framed the house.

Behind the house and off to the side a bit stood the barn. In front was a man shoeing a horse, and another was using a pitchfork to load hay into one of the stalls inside. Ana could also see someone heading toward the back of the barn and toward a long wooden building she thought might be a bunkhouse.

Josie led them up onto the porch, where two Indian men were waiting.

"Girls, I would like you to meet Howling Wolf and his son, Little Bear."

The oldest of the two smiled while the younger gave an exaggerated roll of his eyes.

"She likes using our Indian names whenever possible," Howling Wolf said with a grin.

"Those are your given names, are they not?"

As the two exchanged teasing looks, Little Bear spoke, "Those *are* our given names, but folks around here call Pa *Joe* and call me—"

"A pain," his father said, turning the teasing his way.

Ana liked these two already.

"Noah. You can call me Noah," the younger man said as he and his pa traded playful punches on each other's arms.

"These two are constantly going at it like this. So you should pay no never mind to either of them." Josie gave them both a playful swat of her own.

"Joe, Noah, I would like you both to meet my nieces. This is Ana Grace, and this little lady is Lucy."

Both men tipped their hats then waited for the next introduction.

"This is Mr. Thomas Schneider. The girl's father hired him to be their escort. He's decided to stay with us for a while, so the guesthouse will need to be stocked."

The men exchanged handshakes as Thomas spoke, "Please, call me Thomas." He made sure Josie knew he meant her as well with a nod in her direction.

Josie continued, "Joe has been my ranch manager for about fifteen years now. Noah helps wherever we need him. And right now, he needs to gather your things from the wagon."

Noah headed off the porch, but not before flashing a huge smile. He was tall and lanky, and Ana figured him to be in his early to midtwenties. His dark skin and hair were both typical of all the Indians she had ever seen portrayed in paintings or picture books. He wore his hair long and had small braids on either side of his face.

Ana realized his father's was fashioned the same way. Joe's, however, had already grayed quite a bit. He was somewhat shorter than his son and a little more robust, but the family resemblance was definitely a strong one.

"Joe, could you please take Mr. Schneider and show him the guesthouse. Let him get settled then head back up here, and we will have an early lunch."

"Yes, ma'am," Joe said, and then he and Thomas headed off the porch and toward the rear of the house.

Josie led the girls inside the house and began to show them around. They started in the sitting room. Ana was surprised to discover that the interior decor of the house was light and cheerful despite the rugged exterior. Pastels found in the window coverings and upholstery were a pleasant contrast to the clean-white walls.

Josie led them into the rest of the rooms, filling them in on the history of certain items. They made their way upstairs to a bedroom Josie informed Lucy was hers. Ana's was straight across the hall.

Lucy's room had a view of the rolling hills behind the house while Ana's looked out toward the beautiful lavender fields in the front. Both rooms had windows on the end that gave a view of the corrals and the barn. Ana couldn't believe they were able to have their own rooms. They had never had their own rooms!

"You girls would probably like to wash up and maybe change out of those gritty clothes, so I will leave you to it. You will find freshwater in the pitchers and linens located on the washstands in both rooms. Head on down to the kitchen when you're ready." Tears began to fill Josie's eyes. "I'm so glad you are here."

They exchanged smiles, and Josie made her leave. Noah appeared carrying one of Ana and Lucy's trunks as she was exiting the room.

"Where would you like this?" Noah asked.

"Oh, at the end of the bed would be fine," Ana instructed. "Thank you for bringing it up."

"No problem," he said before heading back out the door and down the stairs.

Ana locked the bedroom door and went to the trunk for fresh clothes. She saw the gift they had gotten for Josie as soon as she opened the trunk.

"I had forgotten about this." Ana pulled the package from its hiding place.

"Me too! I want to go give it to her now!" Lucy exclaimed, grabbed her hand, and started tugging.

"We need to clean up first. We can give it to her when we go down to eat lunch."

"Okay, let's hurry!"

Ana quickly helped Lucy change into some clean clothes and then took a stab at washing some of the grime off her face and hands. She then undid the braids in her sister's hair, gave it a good brushing, and replaced the braids.

Lucy had dark-blonde hair, matching their papa's, which reached all the way to the small of her back. Their father had always refused to allow Liza to cut it, so to keep it somewhat tamed, it was kept in braids most of the time.

They stood in front of the mirror as Ana worked on Lucy's hair. As she brushed, she became envious, as she did every time, at how easily Lucy's long straight hair was to manage. Her own hair was a mass of curls and always seemed to have a mind of its own.

Ana noticed Lucy had her blue eyes, also like their papa's, fixed on an opened window where the sounds of the corral flowed into the room. She had a good feeling her sister would become a regular fixture out there since Lucy loved horses.

Lucy waited impatiently as Ana tidied herself. Once presentable, they quickly headed down the stairs and toward the kitchen, a wonderful aroma leading the way.

Josie turned from her spot in front of the stove and then looked at the gift Lucy had insisted on carrying. Lucy walked toward her and held out the package.

"This is for you. I helped pick it out."

"You did? Why, thank you so much, but you didn't have to get me a gift."

"We wanted to get you a little something to thank you for letting us come," Ana told her.

"No thanks necessary." She took the gift and sat at the kitchen table and began to open it.

She untied the ribbon, laid it to the side, and began to unfold the fabric. Once the fabric was gone, she removed the lid and pulled out the straw covering the treasure. "Oh my! Girls, this is the most beautiful piece I have ever seen!"

"We're pleased you like it." Ana beamed.

At that moment, Joe and Thomas entered through the back door.

"Joe, look what the girls brought me! Isn't it beautiful?" Josie exclaimed.

"Yes, it is at that," he said as he took in the details of the glass piece.

Josie sat the candle and candlestick in the middle of the table with a promise to find a perfect place for it later. She then came over to Ana and Lucy and gave them both a hug before going back to her soup on the stove. Ana caught her several times reaching to wipe a stray tear.

They spent the meal filling one another in on their lives, and then Josie led them on a walk around the ranch. After introducing them to several of the ranch hands, she then showed them the guesthouse where Thomas would be staying.

They walked past the bunkhouse where the ranch hands stayed and then on to two tiny houses sitting back away from all the other buildings. A woman was sitting on the porch of one of the houses, and Josie led them toward her.

"I want to introduce you to someone else."

"Hello, Josie," the woman greeted as they reached the pathway to the house.

"Hello, I brought someone for you to meet."

"Wonderful! I was hoping I would get to see them today."

"Sarah, these are my nieces, Ana and Lucy," Josie announced with pride as they made their way onto the porch. "Girls, this is Sarah, Joe's wife, and of course, Noah's mother."

"It's nice to meet you." Ana was amazed at how much Noah favored both his parents.

"It's nice to meet you," Lucy shyly offered her greeting.

"It's a pleasure to finally meet the two of you. Your Aunt Josie has been on pins and needles ever since she heard you were coming. She also informed me of the tragedies you faced while on your journey, and I am so very sorry for it."

"Thank you." Ana was touched by the sincerity in the older woman's voice.

A younger Indian woman came out of the house carrying the most adorable baby Ana had ever seen.

"Elisabeth, these are Josie's nieces, Ana and Lucy," Sarah informed her.

"Oh, hello," the woman said as she juggled the wiggly infant to her *other* hip.

"She is married to Noah, and that is their little boy, Isaiah. He is the sweetest thing you'll ever meet, I assure you," Josie added.

Isaiah let out a squeal as if in agreement, causing all of them to laugh. Lucy walked up and began playing with him. This caused him to giggle and bounce up and down on his mother's hip even more than he already was.

"I can tell you two will be best of friends," Elisabeth told Lucy. "He really likes you."

"Yes, he does. May I come and play with him tomorrow?"

"You may come and play with Isaiah anytime as long as it is okay with Ana and your Aunt Josie, of course."

Lucy seemed fine with this and continued to play with the baby until Josie announced it was time to be moving on.

"I'll see you tomorrow, baby Isaiah," Lucy told him as she went bounding off the porch. She spun around to face the three people on the porch just as she reached the bottom step. "What are your Indian names? Joe and Noah are Howling Wolf and Little Bear. I figured you all had one too."

"Mine is Dancing Winds," Sarah began, "and Elisabeth's is Mourning Dove."

"Isaiah's is Kicking Bear, because he sure did kick a lot before he was born!" his mother told Lucy.

Everyone laughed at this as the little boy wiggled in his mother's arms.

Josie then took them on a horseback ride across the field of lavender to Flint Creek and showed them the swimming hole. She assured the girls that the calm waters, in most places, would probably only come to Lucy's chest. The end of the pool closest to the woods, however, would probably be a little over Ana's head.

"It's not only a good swimming hole, it's good for fishing too," Josie told them. "Joe formed it not long after I hired him. You two can come out here anytime as long as you inform me first."

"I can't wait!" Lucy jumped up and down, emphasizing her excitement.

On the banks alongside the pool were a few big oak, maple, and pine trees. There was also a very large weeping willow. Many of its branches hung out over the water, giving the whole scene a very peaceful feeling. At the base of the willow was a huge rock with a flat surface.

From the rock, one would be able to take in the calming waters of the creek, the rolling hills, the vast lavender fields, and the rustic beauty of the ranch. Ana knew she would be spending a lot of time here, for it had instantly become her favorite spot on the ranch.

Their first day in Flint Creek was ending before Ana knew it. Even though she missed home, she was beginning to look forward to what this new place had in store for her.

9

THE SHRILL NEIGHS of a horse in apparent distress and the shouts of several men woke Ana from a deep sleep the next morning. She flew to her open window to investigate and saw Noah in the middle of the corral atop a black bucking horse. An audience of about six men stood along the corral fence, two of whom she recognized to be Thomas and Joe. Josie and Lucy came from around the corner of the house to watch the show and took a spot alongside the fence as well.

Ana continued to watch from her window, amazed at how brave and strong Noah seemed to be. The horse put everything it had into trying to throw him to the ground, but he bravely kept up the fight.

Every jump and twist of the horse and its rider caused her heart to race. She waited for Noah to lose his battle and go flying through the air at any moment. Amazingly, the horse began to calm, and Noah gained complete control. The onlookers gave a little cheer.

When Josie and Lucy turned to start back toward the house, Lucy spotted her sister in the window. "Did you see that, Ana?"

"Yes, I did."

"Get dressed and come on down," Josie instructed.

Ana ducked back inside to do as she was told. When she reached the bottom of the stairs, she was surprised to see the hands on the grandfather clock indicating it was lunchtime. She could not believe she had slept that late, much less been allowed to. She headed on toward the kitchen, the wonderful aroma of what smelled like beef stew simmering on the stove leading the way.

"I thought you were never going to wake up!" Lucy exclaimed as Ana walked through the door.

"I can't believe I slept so late."

"Aunt Josie said I couldn't wake you." Lucy pouted.

"You should have let her, Josie. There were probably things that I could have been helping you with."

"There will be plenty of things for you to help me do and plenty of time to do it in. I felt you needed the extra rest."

"Thank you. I do feel refreshed. It has been such a long and stressful week."

Josie made her way to Ana's side and wrapped her in a big hug. "I'm so sorry for the things you have had to endure. Not only with this trip but everything."

Ana knew she was referring to her mother. "I have dealt with things rather well, I think."

"You most certainly have. You're a very strong and independent young woman. But I feel that you have lost some of your childhood, and I want to make sure you get a little of it back while you are here with me."

Hearing these words from Josie and seeing the sincerity in her eyes gave Ana a feeling of warmth and contentment she had not felt since her mother passed. All she could do in response was to give her aunt a tight hug of her own.

They were still in their embrace when Thomas came through the back door. "Oh, Ana," he started, "I am glad you are up! Did you sleep well?"

"Yes, I did, thank you. Is that a telegram?" Ana realized he was holding some papers in his hand, and she was instantly hopeful.

"Yes, two actually," he said, opening the first one.

Everyone gathered around the kitchen table as Thomas read:

> THOMAS SCHNEIDER, FLINT CREEK, TEXAS
>
> GLAD TO HEAR YOU REACHED FLINT CREEK SAFELY—*stop*—FIGHTING STILL SPORADIC IN NORTHEAST—*stop*—MANAGING TO CONTROL BEST SUPPLY ROUTES—*stop*—SERGEANT DALTON IN SHREVEPORT HELPING WITH INVESTIGATION—*stop*—WILL BE IN TOUCH WITH NEWS ASAP—*stop*
>
> COLONEL JAMES LAWSON

"It sounds like things are a little better back home," Josie said in her attempt to comfort a crying Lucy.

"I miss Papa!" Lucy cried.

"I know you do, honey." She scooped Lucy up into her arms.

"What is the other telegram, Thomas?" Ana's curiosity was piqued.

"It's actually a telegram addressed to you."

Puzzled, Ana took it from him and was surprised to see it was from Jacob. She looked to find Thomas with a teasing grin on his face. Her cheeks flamed in embarrassment as she took the paper from Thomas. She asked to be excused and then headed out the back door and around to the swing hanging from the oak tree out front.

Once there, she took a seat, opened the missive, and began to take in the words in front of her.

> ANA GRACE LAWSON, FLINT CREEK, TEXAS
>
> IN SHREVEPORT LOOKING INTO CASE—*stop*—ALREADY HAVE LEADS—*stop*—SEND CORRESPONDENCE TO ME HERE—*stop*—HOPE TO HEAR FROM YOU SOON
>
> JACOB DALTON

Ana closed the note, knowing in her heart what Jacob said was true. Those men were going to pay for what they did to her sweet Liza. Jacob would make sure of it. Ana's heart also did funny things with the knowledge he did indeed want her to write to him.

When he mentioned it on the train, she figured he was only being nice, but he really expected to hear from her. Ana would have to ask Josie for some supplies so she could get a letter off to him as soon as possible.

Ana went back inside feeling more than a tad bit giddy. Luckily, she was able to get her emotions under control before anyone noticed—or so she thought. During the meal, Ana kept noticing Josie watching her. She felt sure her aunt would be questioning her later.

The meal ended, and Lucy asked Thomas to take her out on horseback.

"Only if Josie says it's okay," Thomas said.

"May we please, Aunt Josie?"

"That's a wonderful idea! You should take a couple of fishing poles with you and try your luck down at the creek," Josie suggested.

"Can we, Thomas?"

"Sure, sounds like fun! Where can we find the poles, Josie?"

"Out in the barn, first door on the right. You'll also find a small spade to dig for worms and a coffee tin to carry them in."

"Great! You ready, Lucy?" Thomas asked, all the while knowing the answer he was going to get.

"Yes, yes, yes!" Lucy squealed as she began to drag a laughing Thomas toward the door.

"Would you like to go too, Ana?" Thomas managed to ask before Lucy pulled him out the door.

"No, not this time. I have some things I want to do." She had every intention getting some writing done.

With that, they were out the door and on their way, but not before Thomas and Josie shared a little smile, which sent Ana's mind racing.

What was that all about?

Ana looked to Josie and saw that she still had a small grin on her face. "What are you grinning about, Josie?"

"What makes you think I am grinning about anything? Can I not be grinning because I feel like grinning?"

Her defensive behavior caused Ana to laugh. "It sounds like the lady doth protest too much," Ana quoted a play that she had read once.

Josie gave her a funny look but turned and went back to the dishes they were washing together. Ana decided to let the matter drop, at least for now. She decided to ask about the writing supplies she needed instead.

"Josie, do you have any supplies I could use to write a letter?"

"Yes, of course. They are in the roll top in the living room. Feel free to take what you need." She stopped what she was doing and looked at the younger girl. "There is some fancy paper and envelopes in the top drawer, if the letter needs to be a little more special."

This caused Ana to stop drying the plate she was working on and look at Josie. It was obvious she was intent on some teasing of her own by the twinkle in her eyes. "What?"

"The telegram you received. It was from that solider who helped get you out of Chattanooga, right?"

"Yes." Ana could feel the heat rise in her face once again. Josie had figured her out.

"Well…" Josie let the word hang in the air, clearly wanting her to go on. "Listen, it's all right if you don't want to talk about it. Thomas told me Dalton was a godsend during that time. And he was the one your father sent to Louisiana to look for the men who killed Liza. He also said he believed Dalton to be a very good and upstanding young man. Thomas also told me he overheard you two talking about writing each other. It really is all right with me."

Josie paused, looking a little frustrated. "I know I am rambling, and I'm sorry. I have never had kids of my own or been around any as they were growing up, except for Noah."

Ana put her hand over her mouth in an attempt to hide her laughter from her aunt. When Josie realized what she was doing, she started to giggle herself.

"I am sorry," Josie said.

"Don't be."

"No, really, I'm not used to all of this. I want you to feel you can talk to me, and here I am rambling on like a daft woman. Your mother would not be pleased."

"Mother would most definitely be pleased, Josie. Knowing we are here with you probably has her dancing in the streets in heaven. She used to talk about you all the time. She always had plans for us to be together someday." This thought caused a lump to form in Ana's throat and tears to form in both her and her aunt's eyes.

"You sound exactly like her when you talk, did you know that? You are like her in so many ways, and I have no doubts she is so proud of you. I want to make her proud of me too by taking care of her girls precisely as she would," Josie said.

"Oh, Josie."

The two cried on each other's shoulder, and when the embrace was over, Josie spoke, "Listen, I don't want to meddle, but I was serious about wanting you to feel free to talk to me." She wiped the tears from Ana's cheek.

"It would be nice to have someone to talk to. So, since you offered…," Ana finished with a sheepish grin.

A big smile crossed Josie's face, and she grabbed Ana's hand and started leading her to the sitting room. "Oh, wait! How about we get ourselves a glass of lemonade and maybe a plate of those cookies Sarah sent over?"

Ana could tell she was excited, so she played along, still a little unsure of opening up to anyone. They loaded a tray with lemonade and cookies and then made their way to the sitting room, each taking a seat on Josie's light-blue sofa. Josie looked at Ana with anticipation. Ana took a deep breath. She began her story.

"When I was first introduced to Jacob, I figured him to be like all the other soldiers I had met. I did think him to be handsome, but I wouldn't allow myself to think on it any further—that is, until we were on the train. I saw the way he handled himself when the Yankees began shooting at the train."

Josie gasped, and Ana realized she didn't know the whole story.

Ana filled her in on all the details, from the time her father told them he was sending them away to their arrival in Flint Creek. The talk went from there to everything else they could think of.

They talked until they both realized it was almost suppertime. Ending the conversation, they headed to the kitchen and began the evening meal. The two of them promised today was only the beginning of many talks together.

Ana thought it felt good to have someone with whom she could talk. She didn't have anyone since her mother passed. Yes, there was Liza, but Ana never felt like she could open up to her the way she had her mother.

Ana had a few friends but, with her father being gone most of the time, didn't spend time with them outside of school. Having Josie was the best thing ever.

They finished with supper a little while later, and Ana headed back to the sitting room to collect paper, ink, and a pen. She then excused herself to her room to begin the letter she had waited all afternoon to write.

10

September 1, 1863
Shreveport, Louisiana

"Dalton, we got a lead on the Murphy gang," Sheriff Jones announced as he sat down at the table. "Source says they are holed up in a cabin down by Caddo Lake."

"Great!" Jacob said over his meal. "How quick can we get a posse together and head out there?"

"I already have plenty of men lined up. They're all over at the saloon waiting on us."

"How reliable is this source?"

"Very. He spotted the gang about a mile outside of town two hours ago and followed them to the lake. He watched them for a while to make sure they were planning to stay and then headed back here with the news."

"Let me pay for my meal, and we will be on our way." Jacob began to wave down the waiter.

"Nonsense." The older man waved him off as the waiter walked up to the table. "Bill, put this gentleman's meal on my tab, will ya?"

"Will do," the waiter said and then turned to leave.

"You don't have to do that," Jacob told the sheriff.

"Ah, don't worry about it. No time for fussin'. We got a job to do."

They then made their way out of the restaurant and down Main Street toward the saloon. A group of about fifteen men, all of them carrying guns and looking ready for a fight, met them when they went inside.

"Dalton," Jones began the introductions, "this is my boy, Seth. He is not only my son, he is one of the best deputies I have ever had, very capable and smart. He is the source I was telling you about. Seth, this is Jacob Dalton."

The two men exchanged handshakes, and the rest of the introductions followed. Most of the others were simply family men fed up with the way the Murphy gang had been terrorizing the town. They were all in the same mind-set. They had to stop these men!

All the men agreed it would be best to wait until way after dark before heading out. A couple of men headed to the hideout to keep watch while the rest waited in the saloon. Jacob was very uncomfortable being anywhere close to that place, however, and decided there was something more constructive he wanted to do with his time.

"Sheriff, I am going to head down to the post office for a bit. Send someone after me if anything changes."

"You got it."

Jacob made his way out onto the boardwalk and started toward the middle of town. He wanted to see if the postmaster had anything for him.

As soon as he stepped into the post office, the man behind the counter stood and headed his way. "You Dalton?" the man asked. "Jacob Dalton?"

"Yes." Jacob wondered how he knew.

"I thought so. The sheriff was in here late yesterday saying someone was coming to help find the Murphy gang. Since I ain't never seen you before, I figured you were the man."

"Sheriff told you about me, huh?" Jacob was not happy the sheriff was spreading their plans around town. That is the last thing they needed, someone to tip off the gang with loose lips.

"Yeah, the sheriff is my brother-in-law and knew I would be glad to know the trash who burned down my barn and stole my horses was about to be brought to justice."

Jacob felt the tension in his shoulders begin to ease.

"Oh yeah, this is for you." He held out an envelope. "I was about to forget all about it!"

Jacob took it from him, thanked him, and then reassured him they would be bringing the gang in soon. He then took his leave and headed to the center of town, taking a seat underneath a huge elm tree. He sat looking at the neat handwriting on the envelope, smiled, and then gently opened the letter and took in the elegantly written words.

Jacob,

How are you doing? Things are going well here. I did not think I would like it here, but I do. Aunt Jose is wonderful! She reminds me so much of Mama. It makes me miss her so much. However, I know in my heart that Mama is happy we have finally met and are getting to know each other.

The ranch is beautiful! So much to see and do! You will have to come for a visit and see for yourself. Having grown up on a farm, I feel you would love it here too! Aunt Jose has already said you would be welcome here anytime.

Lucy is having the time of her life! She is going full out from sunup until sundown! She has everyone here eating out of the palm of her hand, including Thomas. Oh, he decided to stay on at the ranch too!

Aunt Josie has a spare house on the property and insisted Thomas stay for a while. If truth be told, I think he and Josie have an eye for each other. They would probably both berate me if they knew I had even thought such a thing. Oh well, time will tell, I guess.

The last thing I heard from Papa was not good news. He sent us a telegram and told us there was still shelling going on around town. Worst of all, our home has been destroyed in the process! I am trying my best not to even think on it for fear of getting upset. If you have any more information, please let me know.

I wanted to tell you how truly thankful I am you are working on bringing those men to justice. They deserve the worst the law has to offer for what they did to my dear Liza. Whatever you do, please be careful! They are horrible men, and they would not think twice about putting a bullet into you! You cannot let that happen!

Please keep me updated on everything—and thank you again.

Ana Grace Lawson

P.S. Write back soon!

Jacob sat for a moment, letting the words sink in. He was so happy both girls were doing well in Texas. He then reflected on what they had had to go through to get there. He so hoped the next few hours went well, and he would be able to report to them that the men who had killed Liza were in custody. He was going to do his part, that was for sure!

A little while later, Jacob made his way back to the saloon to wait with the others. News arrived not long after sundown that the gang was still at the cabin. Sheriff Jones and Jacob decided it was time to move out. Jacob paused as the men checked their weapons and made their way out to their horses to say a silent prayer for the mission. He prayed God would help them in bringing these men in and that no lives would be lost in the process.

"Now, remember, boys," Jones started, "we're headed out to serve a search warrant. But knowing that bunch, we *do* expect there to trouble. Stay alert and follow my lead. We don't want anybody gettin' their killin' out there tonight."

The ride out to the area where the cabin stood was a quiet, somber one. Everyone seemed focused on the task that lay ahead, which was fine with Jacob as it gave him even more time to spend with the Lord. He so wanted this to go well for everyone's sake.

Jones raised his arm, signaling for everyone to stop. He then turned and, with a wave of his hand, began sending the men off in different directions. He wanted to make sure he had the place surrounded.

Jacob stayed with Jones and his deputy. They climbed down from their horses and secured their reins before making their way through the trees. Jacob was completely lost in the darkness and relied solely on the guidance of the other two men.

He was concentrating so hard on making it through the brush without falling that he didn't notice the sheriff and Seth had stopped. Seth grabbed his arm, bringing him to a halt. He then realized they were at the top of a large hill looking down over the cabin.

They ducked down behind some fallen timber to watch and wait. All around the perimeter began a chorus of chirps and calls. Jones answered back, and then all went quiet. Jones looked at his pocket watch and gave Jacob and Seth a nod.

The plan was for everyone to settle into position and give their signal. Then they would wait for exactly five minutes before moving in. Those next five minutes seemed like an eternity. Jacob's apprehension seemed to intensify with each passing second.

Jacob sat, taking in the scene in front of him. He could see movement inside the cabin and was able to account for the entire gang. At one point, one of the men stepped out onto the front porch. He walked over to the railing, lit a cigar, and after taking a few puffs, started to look around in the darkness as though he could sense their presence.

Please, Lord, don't let him realize we are out here!

The man stood there a minute more. After taking a few more puffs from his cigar, he shook his head and headed back inside. The three men exchanged relieved glances, and Jones looked at his watch. "It's time," he whispered.

The three men made their way down the hill, taking care to be as quiet as possible. Jacob could see the rest of the posse closing in as they grew closer to the cabin. *So far, so good.*

Jacob's little group took their place on the porch, making sure not to cross in front of the windows, and readied themselves around the front door. Seth held up a hand and slowly began to raise one finger at a time. When he reached the count of three, he blasted open the door with one hard kick, and he and Jacob rushed in with guns raised.

"Here to serve a search warrant, Jim," the sheriff announced as he made his way inside.

The cabin was swarming with the posse members before the gang even had time to react. They had everyone subdued and accounted for in no time.

"You'll be sorry for this, Jones!" Jim, the leader of the gang, began to swear.

"Oh, really? And exactly what are you going to do about it?"

"You got no grounds to hold me, or any of these men for that matter!" Jim retorted.

"No, I think you are wrong about that," Jacob said as he held up a blue crocheted shawl he found crumpled up in the corner of the room.

"That ain't nothin'!" Jim barked.

All in the room could feel the fury that flew through Jacob. Everyone seemed to tense, as if waiting for the explosion they were sure was about to come. Jacob was right up in Jim's face in one swift movement.

"Nothing, huh?" Jacob growled through clenched teeth.

"Ye…yeah," Jim stuttered, suddenly not as big and brave as he thought he was. "Just something we found ou…out in the woods."

"Really?"

"Ye…yeah, I swear!"

Jacob grabbed the lowlife around the neck with both hands and lifted him clear off the floor. "You sure about that?" he asked, still sounding more like a grizzly bear than a man.

Jim struggled to breath, his face growing redder by the second. Jacob was unrelenting. He kept holding him up in the air until finally Jim squeaked out a barely audible, "O... kay!"

Jacob dropped him on the floor in a heap. Jim coughed and sputtered, trying to get air back into his lungs. Finally managing to suck in a big gulp of air, he made the worst mistake of the evening.

He turned his blood-red, oxygen-starved face toward Jacob and said, "She was only a stupid nigger!"

Those turned out to be the last words Jim spoke that night.

Back in town the next day, Jacob helped with his part of the paperwork in the sheriff's office. He also contacted the marshall to let him know they had captured the gang. The marshall assured him a wagon was already on the way to gather them up to take them to the federal pen.

All the men admitted to the crimes to which they were charged, crimes ranging from burglary to bank robbery to murder. They would be in prison for a very long time unless the judge sentenced them to hang. Jacob secretly hoped that would be the case.

He knew it was wrong of him to feel that way, and he would need to repent. Right now, however, he struggled with the rage inside him over what they did to Ana, Lucy, Thomas, and poor Liza. His only consolation was he was going to be able to report to Ana that the men were in custody.

As he finished signing the last paper, he looked to Sheriff Jones and Seth. "I don't know how to thank you gentlemen."

"No thanks necessary," Seth assured him.

"Yeah, we should be thanking you. We have been trying to get enough on those reprobates to bring 'em in for a long time. I truly hate what happened to your friend, but rest assured they won't be hurtin' nobody else," Jones told him.

"When will the marshall's wagon be here?" Seth asked.

"They should be here first thing in the morning," Jacob told him. "I plan to see the prisoners on the wagon, and then I am headed south."

"I was hoping I could talk you into staying around here. I think the three of us make a pretty good team," Jones said hopefully.

"We do, indeed," Jacob began, "but I want to deliver this bit of good news to Liza's family in person. Then I have to get back to the army. Don't want 'em to think I have gone AWOL!" He finished with a laugh.

The other men joined in, and Seth reached out his hand to Jacob. "Well, I hope you will at least come back through here sometime."

Jacob took his outstretched hand. "That you can count on! I will see you gentlemen in the morning. The wagon should be in about nine." Jacob turned to shake the sheriff's hand as well and headed out of the office and toward the hotel.

The next morning was uneventful as all the men were loaded onto the wagon without incident. Jacob felt sure Jim would try to act up again, but thankfully, he didn't. He barely took his eyes off his feet as Seth led him from his jail cell to the guards waiting to take him to prison.

Jacob said his good-byes as soon as the prison wagon was out of sight and headed to the depot and the train that would take him to Texas.

11

September 7, 1863

ANA AWOKE AND dressed for the day. But before heading downstairs to breakfast, she got on her knees to have her morning talk with God. Ana was amazed at how quickly she was growing accustomed to this routine. She was even more amazed at how easy praying was becoming.

After Liza died, she didn't think she would ever want to talk to Him again. Jacob's words kept echoing through her mind, however, so she decided to give Him another chance. She was pleased to discover it did make things easier.

Ana reached the kitchen about the same time as Josie, and they began to work in harmony on the morning meal. It didn't take long for the smell of bacon to reach the hungry noses of Thomas and Lucy. They each made an appearance at the door even before the first layer came out of the skillet.

Breakfast passed with little excitement. Ana and Josie finished with the cleanup and then readied a large roast for the oven. Ana started peeling potatoes and carrots to go around it as Josie seasoned the meat. They added everything to a large Dutch oven, and then Josie slid it into the black cast-iron cookstove.

Josie then headed out to the barn to begin her morning chores while Ana headed back upstairs to take care of a few of her own. She had neglected Lucy's and her room since they had gotten there and had made Josie the promise she would get them both in order this morning.

Starting with Lucy's room, Ana worked quickly and, in no time, had both rooms looking spotless. Everything was in its place, and no dust could be seen anywhere. She did, however, notice a few streaks on a couple of the windowpanes in her own room. She grabbed her cleaning cloth and began to rub.

Once Ana was sure she had the glass sparkling clean, she stood back to admire her work and to admire the wonderful lavender view it provided her. She realized, as she stood looking at the beautiful purple flowers, that there was a rider headed up the long trail leading to the house.

She found something familiar in the rider as she watched him atop his horse. Her eyes finally focused on the man, and her heart leapt with the realization of who he was. Ana became light-headed and realized she was holding her breath.

She let it out in a rush. "Jacob!"

No sooner had his name crossed her lips than she heard her sister let out a squeal. Lucy raced around the end of the house to meet Jacob as he was coming off his horse. They shared a hug and then began making their way toward the front porch. The sight of him getting closer to the house caused Ana to panic.

Ana remembered she had been cleaning and knew she must look dreadful. She rushed to the dresser and started removing the bun from her hair she had fixed earlier. She opted to replace it with a loose chignon and worked quickly to get it pinned in place. Once satisfied, she spun to head downstairs and saw Josie watching her from the doorway.

"I was coming to tell you, you had company, but I see you already know."

"I can't believe he is here." Ana was breathless. "I wonder if this means he was able to catch the men that killed Liza."

"I don't know. Why not head downstairs and find out?"

"I had to clean up a little first. Is this dress all right?" Ana examined herself in the full-length mirror.

"Your dress is fine."

"It's not suitable for company. I have to change."

Ana raced to her wardrobe and flung open the doors. She skimmed through her selection of dresses and quickly settled on a simple light-pink day dress. The fabric had a scattering of dark-pink flowers, a white lace collar, and was one of the few dresses she had that did not require a hoop.

Josie helped her change and stood in her wake as she rushed from the room and toward the stairs.

Lucy already had Jacob on the porch, torturing him with facts about the ranch, by the time Ana made it downstairs. Thomas stood helplessly by, waiting for his turn to join in the conversation. Ana knew someone needed to rescue Jacob fast, or Lucy would have him completely worn out in no time.

"Lucy, do you not ever take a breath?" Ana asked sarcastically as she stepped through the screen door and made her way across the porch. Lucy gave her big sister a dirty look but stopped her attack on poor Jacob.

Jacob looked at Ana and smiled, and all she could do was smile in return. Thomas had to pretend to clear his throat to break the spell.

"Hello, Ana Grace."

"Hello, Jacob." Ana began trying to tame some of the loose curls that were dancing in the breeze around her face.

"It's good to see you," he said as he made his way to stand in front of her.

"It's good to see you too. I would like for you to meet my Aunt Josie."

"Pleasure to meet you, ma'am." He gave a slight nod of his head.

"Nice to meet you too, Jacob."

"Ana's birthday is in a few days!" Lucy announced after placing herself neatly in the center of everyone.

"Oh, really?" Jacob's eyes made their way back to Ana.

"Yeah, it's no big deal," Ana said, trying to sound nonchalant.

"I think all birthdays are a big deal." Jacob grinned. "What day is it, exactly?"

"Saturday, the ninth," Lucy answered his question before Ana could.

"Well, that is great! I'll not be leaving until Sunday, so I can join in the celebration."

"Yay!" Lucy began bouncing up and down.

Everyone laughed at Lucy's enthusiasm as they watched her bound off the porch and head back around the side of the house.

Jacob's mood then became serious. Ana knew in her heart why he was here and could wait no longer to hear all about it.

"Jacob?" Anticipation was evident in her whispered voice.

"Let's all take a seat," Josie said as she began pulling the rockers closer together.

He looked long and hard into Ana's eyes after everyone sat down. "It's all over, Ana. We got 'em."

These were the words Ana felt as though she had waited on forever! Her hand went to her mouth as the tears began to fall. She instantly found herself wrapped in Josie's arms. Thomas and Jacob sat back and allowed her to let go of the emotions she had been holding on to so tightly.

Ana was able to regain control of her emotions long enough to ask, "Where are they now?"

"It turns out the list of their crimes was very extensive. They were hung for those crimes two days ago."

These words caused another torrent of tears. It was really over! They could hurt no one else!

It felt good to be able to release all those feelings trapped inside ever since that horrible day. Ana's need to be strong for Lucy's sake had not allowed her to grieve as she needed to. She now held nothing back.

Ana felt an amazing peace once she had shed all her tears. She now knew everything was going to be okay. She also knew she needed to hear the whole story.

"I want to know everything, Jacob. I want to hear every last detail of their capture." Her voice was still shaky.

"Are you sure?"

"Yes, I am sure."

Jacob spent the next hour giving his account of the events leading up to the end of the gang's reign of terror. His audience listened in amazement as Jacob shared his story. All were very relieved to learn no one in the group received any injuries. Ana felt Jacob was holding back some of the details but realized she probably didn't want to hear them anyway.

"Jacob, you must be worn out from your journey," Josie stated then turned to Thomas. "Would you mind taking Jacob around to the guesthouse so he can freshen up?"

"That's a great idea," Thomas said as he stood and then motioned for Jacob to follow.

Jacob stood and addressed Josie, "I really appreciate it, but I actually got into town late last night and was able to clean up and get a good night's sleep before I headed out here."

"Well, okay then. You aren't still holding on to that room, are you?"

Ana and Thomas knew exactly what was coming and shared a little smile.

"Well…yes. I figured I would hang around here for the afternoon, if that's all right, and then head back into town before dark."

Josie was waving her hand in protest before he even finished the sentence. "Nonsense, you will stay here," she told him in her matter-of-fact way and then stood and headed for the front steps. "I will get Noah to head into town and collect your things."

"You really don't have to do that. The room at the hotel is fine."

"I'm sure it is, but it lacks family," Josie finished her descent and headed around the side of the house, her mind clearly made up.

Ana and Thomas began to giggle, and Jacob looked to each of them with a bewildered expression. He then replaced it quickly with one of his wonderful smiles. "Looks like I am staying here!"

They all burst out with laughter.

They spent the rest of the morning on a tour of the ranch. Lucy had rejoined them and did most of the teaching. She was so excited and made sure she pointed out every little detail, right down to the spiderweb belonging to a writing spider she had named Spot. Ana assumed she had come up with the name because of the black spots on the spider's bright-yellow body.

Before they knew it, it was time for lunch.

Lucy started begging Josie for a picnic as they reached the kitchen door. "Jacob needs to picnic down by the swimming hole!" she explained to Josie.

Josie looked to Ana and Jacob, and they both shrugged their shoulders.

"That's fine with me, if it's not too much trouble for you," Jacob told Josie.

"No trouble at all. Ana, grab the basket out of the pantry."

As Ana turned to head that way, Josie began wrapping the biscuits and ham they had left over from breakfast. Ana sat the basket down and began packing it. By the time they were finished, they had added fresh buttermilk pie, apples, carrots, and a couple jars of fresh lemonade. Jacob took the basket, and the picnickers headed for the door.

After a short walk through the lavender meadow, they set up their little feast on the huge flat rock on the edge of the swimming hole. Sounds of nature surrounded them while they ate in silence, and Ana allowed the peaceful sounds to soothe her troubled spirit. Ana asked the other question that had been on her mind since Jacob's arrival as soon as they finished eating.

"Have you heard from my father? Are they still fighting around Chattanooga?"

"Yes and yes. That's all I do know, though—except that your father is still doing well."

Ana nodded and began to repack the basket as Lucy took over the conversation. She went on and on telling (or retelling) Jacob things about the ranch. Ana allowed her to walk barefoot along the edge of the pool once she had finished her barrage of information.

"Are you okay?" Jacob asked once Lucy was out of earshot.

"Yes, why do you ask?"

"You've been through so much." He skipped a stone across the water.

"I'm okay."

He looked at her for a long moment before he spoke, "You know, I really believe you are. I mean, you are probably the strongest and bravest woman I have ever known." He then turned to skip another stone.

Ana could feel the blood rush to her cheeks. *He called me a woman. Was he trying to be nice, or does he really see me that way?*

Ana was glad his back was to her so he could not see the emotions she was sure were playing across her face.

Supper turned into a big event. Josie had invited Joe and his whole family in honor of Jacob's arrival and the news he brought. Sarah and Elisabeth—or Beth as she had asked them to call her—had baked bread and a cake for the occasion. Josie had added a huge pot of beans and greens to her already hearty menu of beef roast and vegetables.

The atmosphere was light and cheerful, and everyone had a wonderful time. Jacob seemed to fit in perfectly with the entire group, but he and Noah hit it off best. In no time at all, they acted as though they had known each other forever.

After supper, Joe and his family began to make their way toward home, but not before Noah promised Jacob he would take him out on horseback the next day to show him the rest of the land.

Beth then asked Ana to babysit in the morning so she could go into town. Ana could not wait to get to take care of little Isaiah. He was such a wonderful baby and so much fun to play with.

"I would love to!" Ana exclaimed.

"Wonderful! I have a few things I really need to get done, and it would be so much easier without him on my hip," Beth explained.

"Of course, anytime you need me. I am always willing to take care of this little man." Ana reached and tickled Isaiah's tiny foot swinging at his mother's side.

"Me too! May I help?" Lucy pleaded. "I'll do a great job, I promise!"

"You can come too, if Ana says it's all right," Beth said.

"That would be wonderful. I could probably use your help," Ana told her little sister.

This seemed to make Lucy's day, and she bounced up and down, clapping her hands. After a quick kiss to Isaiah's head, she went bounding through the house. Ana and Beth shared a laugh, and then Ana reached to give the precious little head a kiss of her own. "See you tomorrow, Isaiah," she told him.

"Say bye-bye," Beth instructed her son as she took his hand and helped him with a wave. They then turned and headed out the back door and down across the yard toward home.

Ana made her way through the house and out onto the front porch, where she found Thomas and Jacob leaning against the railing in deep conversation. They both turned with the sound of the door opening and sent smiles her way. Ana didn't want to disturb their talk, so she walked to the end of the porch, took a seat in the swing, and began watching Lucy out in the yard catching lightning bugs.

Ana was so lost in that scene she didn't realize Jacob had walked up until he sat down beside her and gave her a start.

"Oh—I'm sorry! I really didn't mean to scare you."

"It's all right."

Silence.

"So what do you think of the ranch?"

"It's amazing! There are ranches back home, but nothing like this. Everything seems to work like a well-oiled machine."

"Yes, it does. You and Noah seemed to hit it off."

"I like him. I think we could be really close friends."

"There is no reason why not."

"You're right."

"You could visit anytime you want. Josie wouldn't mind at all."

"It certainly would be nice to visit Hill Country from time to time." Jacob flashed Ana a quick and uncharacteristically shy smile and then quickly began watching Lucy.

Again, silence.

"Oh…uh…I have something for you," he said.

Ana gave him a puzzled look as he began opening the saddlebag she hadn't realized he was carrying. He looked her in the eye as he reached his hand inside and then carefully said, "I would have given this to you earlier, but I wanted to be sure you would be able to handle it first."

Ana was confused until she saw what he pulled from the bag.

"Oh, Jacob," she cried in a whispered voice, "Liza's shawl! How did you…where did…"

He gently brushed a curl away from her wet eyes. "None of that is important."

"Thank you." Ana held her treasure tightly to her chest.

Jacob stood to leave, thinking Ana needed to be alone, but she stopped him with a quick grab of his hand. He sat back down beside her on the swing. They sat there, silent, offering each other nothing except each other's company.

Lucy, tired of her hunting, came to the porch to show them the ones she had caught. Jacob then began to play with her and her collection, leaving Ana to her thoughts.

Ana couldn't believe where her life had gone in such a short time. She imagined Liza working each stitch as she ran her hand across the weathered blue shawl. Her heart skipped, and a tear escaped and made its way down her cheek.

She then thought of her father and then of her beautiful home. A hateful war had taken it and could quite possibly take even more from her.

Ana's thoughts then drifted to her mother. She missed her so much! Ana closed her eyes only for a moment, but in that moment, she was there. The vision in her mind was so vivid she could almost swear it was real.

My sweet baby girl. Open your eyes and look at the blessings you have in front of you. Ana did as the vision of her mother instructed.

There, before her, Josie and Thomas laughed at each other's silly jokes. The fact they were falling for each other was becoming more and more obvious. On the porch floor were Josie's two collies, Hank and Bandit, lovingly attacking Jacob and Lucy. The more they licked, the more Lucy squealed in delight. The more she would squeal, the more Jacob would laugh. He looked up and smiled at Ana right before Bandit knocked him backward, sending Lucy into a fit of laughter. Ana closed her eyes again.

You see, my sweet Ana? Yes, you have had hard, horrible things happen in your short life. But look what is in front of you and the happiness that it all offers. No more sadness, my love.

With that, her mother was gone. Ana opened her eyes and sat in shock at what had just happened. She realized the entire event was only her imagination, but she also realized, with amazement, that it didn't matter.

What mattered was what her mother had said to her: *No more sadness.* That, she could definitely handle. Ana dried her eyes, stood, and wrapped the shawl around her shoulders. She then made her way to her family's side with a smile spreading across her face. It was time for her to get in on the fun!

12

ANA AND LUCY began their walk to Noah and Beth's home the next morning escorted by Jacob. Lucy, of course, thought they were walking way too slowly and set a pace of her own, way out ahead of Jacob and her sister.

"I have wanted to ask all morning." Jacob began. "How are you? I mean, yesterday was pretty eventful. It wasn't too much, was it?"

"What happened to my being the strongest and bravest woman you ever met?" Ana said, causing him to stop dead in his tracks. He turned to face her and smiled when he saw the teasing in her eyes.

Ana spoke as they continued on their way, "It was a lot to take in for one day, but I survived."

"I guess you did. You certainly seem to be in a good mood today."

"I am. I realized something last night."

"What was that?"

"That even though Lucy and I have been through a lot of unhappy things, there are still a lot of happy things out there to be had."

Jacob stopped again and took Ana by the arm, causing her to stand face-to-face with him. He stood looking into her eyes in a way she did not recognize. All she knew was, suddenly, she felt all warm inside. Ana did not know how long they stood that way, but it was over way too soon.

He broke the spell with a soft, sweet smile as he reached up and trapped one of her windblown curls between his fingers. He looked as though he was about to say something. Instead, he turned and began walking again.

"What were you going to say?" Ana asked once she caught up with him.

"Not yet." He smiled and turned his attention back to the trail.

The rest of their walk was in silence. However, the question of what he was about to say burned in Ana's mind and haunted her for the rest of the morning.

"All of this belongs to Josie?" Jacob asked in amazement.

Noah had made good on his promise from the night before and was giving Jacob the grand tour.

"Sure is!" Noah assured him from atop his horse.

They had made their way along Flint Creek to the top of the tallest peak in the area. Noah had pointed in every direction as far as the eye could see and declared the expanse belonged solely to Josie.

"Incredible!"

"There are just over one hundred thousand acres."

"How did she end up with so much land down here, being born and raised in Tennessee like she was?"

"My father says she left home when she was only eighteen and headed west. It had something to do with a big fight with her father. She made it all the way to Amarillo and ran out of money and ended up working in a hotel there as a maid. There, she met Mr. Keller, an up-and-coming cattleman. He was only supposed to be in Amarillo for a few days before heading back to Dallas but ended up staying a few months.

While he was there, he got into a card game with a wealthy rancher and won most of this land. Even though he was a few years older than Josie, they fell quickly in love, and he asked her to marry him. Of course, she did, and they moved down here and took over the ranch. And over the years, it grew," Noah finished his story and adjusted himself in his saddle.

"Remarkable! What happened to Mr. Keller?"

"That's the sad part," Noah began. "They'd been married for about five years when Mr. Keller took ill with the Spanish influenza. Doctors did all they could do. My grandfather was the medicine man of our tribe, and he tried too. Nothing could save him."

"Do they have any children?"

"No, no children."

"It must have been really hard for her. I imagine women ranchers can have a hard time around here. She must have worked really hard to prove herself to have become so successful."

"Yes, she did. Josie has concentrated on nothing except this ranch since Mr. Keller died. That is until she received word from Ana and Lucy's father."

"I guess that was a huge surprise."

"Yes, but a very good one. It's been really good for her to have those girls here...Thomas too," he added with a sly grin.

Jacob returned the smile. "What's up with that anyway?"

Noah chuckled. "Not sure. All I know is Josie has never seemed as happy as she does of late."

"I think it's great!"

"Me too," Noah agreed.

The two sat in silence for the next few minutes, listening to a hawk screeching overhead and taking in the land in front of them.

"What about you and Ana?" Noah asked, breaking the silence.

"Excuse me?"

Noah gave another chuckle. "I think you know exactly what I'm talking about."

Jacob sat quietly for a moment. "We're friends now, right, Noah?"

"Of course!" Noah assured him.

"Well…" Jacob took a deep breath before continuing. "I do have feelings for Ana. I realized there was something special there when we were on the train together."

"So what's the problem?"

"There are a lot of problems, really."

"*I* see no problem."

Jacob took off his hat, wiped his brow, and placed his hat back on his head.

"I do. First, she is so young."

"Seventeen tomorrow, right? You recently turned twenty. Sounds about right to me."

Jacob sat there looking at his new friend and growing a little frustrated. Noah knew he had made his point.

"Second, I don't know if she would welcome my feelings for her."

"She would," Noah simply said as he chewed the piece of straw he held in his teeth.

"How can you be sure?"

"She looks at you in some of the ways Beth looks at me."

"She does?"

Again, a chuckle. "I'm sensing there is a third reason."

After a deep sigh, Jacob went on, "Third is this dang war. I still have obligations. I can't expect her to wait around for me when there is a chance I won't even make it out."

"Don't think that way! You'll be fine, you'll see."

"I sure hope so, but things are heating up pretty good. Come next week, I will be back in the thick of it. Who knows how much longer it'll last."

"All right, so I see your point, I guess. So what are you going to do? Leave without letting her know how you feel?"

"It's the only way."

"It's the least complicated way, maybe, but not necessarily the best way."

"I can't do that to her, Noah. She has been through so much already. If I tell her how I feel and she was to feel the same way and then something was to happen to me, it would be so much harder for her."

"Something tells me that it would be hard, whether she knows or not."

"I have to pray about it some more. At this point, I don't think it would be a good idea to say anything."

"I'll support whatever you decide, Jacob."

"Thanks," Jacob told him as they then turned their horses and began the ride back to the stables. "I mean, it's not like we won't keep in touch when I leave. We have already made promises to write to each other…" he let the sentence trail off. "What's that saying, 'Absence makes the heart grow fonder'?"

Noah turned a smile toward his friend, causing Jacob to share one of his own.

"Isaiah, what in the world do you have now?" Ana spotted her tiny charge sitting under the kitchen table holding an unidentified object in his tiny hands. She moved closer and realized it was a piece of coal from the scuttle on the hearth. "Oh, you little stinker!"

Thankfully, Ana was able to get to him and get the suet-covered treasure from his chubby fingers before he got the black mess all over himself.

This was how Ana and Lucy's morning had gone since his mother left. Isaiah had recently learned to walk and thought it was his duty to explore every inch of the small house. They would get him out of one thing only to turn around and have to get him out of something else.

Lucy had asked to be excused to go to the privy about an hour ago. Ana stepped out to look for her after she had been gone long enough and saw her headed up the trail toward the corral. Ana had been chasing the little *bee* all by herself ever since and had done a pretty good job too!

The front door opened, and his mother walked through just as Ana was cleaning the last speck of coal dust from his fingers. Delighted squeals erupted from little Isaiah, and he started reaching for Beth.

"How did it go?" Beth asked as she took him from Ana.

"Good." Ana didn't lie. She really had enjoyed the whole experience immensely.

"I hope he was no trouble."

"Honestly, he was into everything, but I enjoyed getting to take care of him. I hope you will let me again sometime."

Beth laughed. "I sure will! I appreciate it so much!" She turned her son so she could look into his eyes. "So you were into everything, huh?" Her silly singsong voice caused him to giggle.

At that moment, the front door opened again, and Noah entered, followed by Jacob.

"Well, I am surprised to see you two back so soon," Beth told her husband.

"We're just getting back. I would have loved to stay out longer, but Josie has some things she wants me to get done this afternoon," Noah explained.

"I bet you two are hungry."

"I was hoping you would notice," Noah teased and then reached to take his son.

Ana helped Beth put a small meal on the table. Afterward, they all sat and ate while sharing many stories and laughs. Ana marveled at how *right* it all felt and prayed that there would be many more meals together in the future.

13

"So school starts on Monday? You must be very excited." Jacob was playing a game of "go fish" with Lucy on the floor of the family room not long after lunch.

"Yes! Thomas and Josie took me to meet my teacher the other day." Lucy's excitement was obvious as her face lit up, and she began bouncing up and down on her knees. "Her name is Mrs. Beason, and she showed me where I was going to sit and everything! Give me all your twos."

"Go fish. That's great! I know you will be the best student she has!" Jacob told her, making her smile. "Give me all your kings."

"Awe! You got two of mine! Now I only have three cards left, and you have five! Give me all your queens!" Jacob handed her a card, causing her to squeal.

"I win! I win! I beat you again, Jacob!"

"You sure did! You're very good at this game."

129

"Thank you! I think I am going to go watch Noah put new shoes on Jack. That is Josie's horse."

"Oh…" Jacob acted as though he had no idea.

Lucy took her leave, and Jacob looked at Ana and smiled. She had been watching from the settee while taking care of some much-needed mending.

"She's something else!" Jacob said, laughing.

"That she is."

Jacob pulled himself out of the floor and made himself at home on the other end of the couch. He sat watching Ana. This made her so nervous that she stuck herself with the needle.

"Ouch!"

"Are you all right?"

"Yes."

"Here, let me see." He scooted closer, took her hand, and began to inspect the damaged finger. "I can't even see a spot."

"I told you I was fine." Ana didn't think she could be more nervous. Having him sit so close was causing her heart to run away.

"Where exactly?" He was still trying to see the pinprick.

"There." Ana pointed out the faint red speck.

"Ah…I see it now." Then, ever so gently, he touched his lips to it. "There, that should make it feel better." He sat holding her hand in his until she felt faint.

Suddenly, there was a noise in the kitchen, breaking the spell. He gently placed her hand on her lap and scooted back to the opposite end of the couch, never taking his eyes from hers. She actually had to remind herself to breathe!

"So are you looking forward to school as much as Lucy?" Jacob asked.

"Har…hardly," she choked out.

"This should be your last year, right?"

"Ye…yes, it is." *Get a grip, Ana!* She took a deep breath in an attempt to calm herself. "Actually, I talked to Mrs. Beason the other day as well, and she thinks I can finish up before Christmas."

"That's great! I know *that* has to excite you!"

"Yes, it does! I will be so glad to have schooling behind me." Her nerves finally began to settle.

They sat quietly for a moment.

"I was thinking…," he began.

"Yes?"

"Well…the morning I got here, before I came to the ranch, I ran into the pastor of the church in town. He seemed like a very nice man, very knowledgeable and compassionate. I was thinking I might try to go Sunday morning, you know, before I have to leave. It's been a long time since I have gotten to enjoy a service, and there is no telling when I'll get another chance."

"If that's what you want to do, you should do it."

"I would like it very much if you would consider going with me."

Ana sat there looking at him, not sure how she felt about the request he made. She had not been in church since her mother passed. She had been talking to God lately—a lot actually, thanks to Jacob—but she didn't know if she was ready to go to church.

Yes, Ana decided, she would go if for no other reason than to get to go with Jacob. She wanted to spend as much time with him as possible before he had to leave. After all, she didn't know when she would be able to see him again— or if she ever would.

"I think that would be a fine idea." Ana felt a peace in her decision as soon as she made it.

Jacob smiled.

"Maybe Thomas, Josie, and Lucy will go too," Jacob thought aloud. "I wonder about Noah and his family. How do they believe? Would they consider going too?" The excitement was building in his voice, and Ana was glad she had agreed to go.

"I don't know. You should ask them."

"I think I will."

Jacob was lost in thought for a moment. Ana went back to her mending.

"I should have asked you already, but are you still talking to God like I suggested?"

Ana laid her sewing aside and turned to him. "Yes, I am. I had a really rough time there for a few days, though, after Liza…" Ana could not finish the sentence. Jacob nodded in understanding, and she went on, "I couldn't understand how God would allow something like that to happen. I didn't want any part of Him. But something you said to me on the train kept haunting me. You told me if I would talk to Him, it would make things easier for me. I trusted in that, and it has helped."

He actually had tears in his eyes when Ana looked back up at him. "I am so glad to hear that, Ana."

"Thanks for telling me. It really has meant a lot."

"Oh, Ana Grace, there is so much more I would love to tell you." His eyes reflected the fullness of his heart. The moment wasn't to last, though.

"Ana!" Lucy came running into the room. "Ana, Jacob, come quickly! Cricket is having her baby!" With that, she whirled around and headed back the same way she came.

"Cricket?" Jacob asked, confusion showing on his face.

"Cricket is Beth's horse. They have been expecting this for the past several days," Ana informed him as she put her sewing away.

"Ah yes, Noah told me they had a mare getting ready to foal. I didn't know her name was Cricket, though." He chuckled.

Ana stood motioning toward the door. "Shall we go take a look?"

"Why not?" He rose from the couch and began leading the way. "After all, I have never seen a cricket give birth before."

Laughter tore through her, causing him to laugh as well.

They were still giggling when they reached the stables and made their way up to the fence surrounding the stall where Cricket was lying. Joe and Noah were at her side; and Thomas, Josie, Sarah, Beth, and little Isaiah were watching through the railing. Lucy had climbed to the very top and was leaning over to get as close a look as possible. Ana and Jacob took their place at the railing as well and waited.

The whole thing really was quite amazing! Ana had heard about such things but had never experienced it firsthand. She could not tear her eyes away for one second, even when she felt Jacob inch closer to her and place his hand on the small of her back.

With every push Cricket made, Ana felt her own breath catch. By the time it was over, she would have sworn she was almost as exhausted as Cricket. The sight of that precious little thing beside his mother, trying desperately to stand on those wobbly long legs, was too much. It was the closest thing to a real-life miracle Ana had ever witnessed.

"God is wonderful, is He not?" Jacob whispered in her ear, somehow sensing what she was feeling.

"Yes, yes, He is."

They all stood watching mother and baby a while longer, none of them wanting to lose the moment. Finally they took their leave to let mother and baby get acquainted in peace.

"When can I ride him?" Lucy wanted to know as soon as they were out of the barn.

"Oh, it will be quite a while before he is big enough for that," Beth told her.

"Oh, all right. Can I ride him when he is big enough?"

"Of course."

Isaiah began to fuss.

"Looks like someone has decided he is hungry," his mother pointed out.

"Come, we will get home so you can feed him, and then we will get started on supper," Sarah told her.

They all said their good-byes and headed toward home.

"Thomas, will you take me fishing?" Lucy wanted to know.

"That sounds like a good idea. Let's go get the poles."

"You should bring back enough for supper," Josie suggested. "I haven't started anything yet, and fish sounds pretty good."

"Will do, my Josie," Thomas said with a grin and then took Lucy by the hand and headed toward the shed.

Ana noticed Josie was actually blushing!

"*My Josie*, he said," Ana teased.

"Oh, stop it, Ana!" Josie scolded as she walked past her toward the house.

Jacob was covering his mouth to keep from smiling.

"Josie, what's the matter? He likes you, and you like him. I think it is wonderful!" Ana exclaimed.

Josie stopped dead in her tracks and turned to face her niece. Ana was afraid Josie was mad at her until she saw the silly look on her face. Ana had to cover her own mouth now.

"You do?"

"Of course, I do! I think you two make a perfect couple. I have since we got here."

"Oh! I am too old for this!" Josie whirled around and continued her trek toward the house.

"Nonsense!" Ana tried, but Josie waved her off and kept walking.

"Josie, you deserve to be happy. And if loving Thomas is part of it, then you shouldn't hold back."

Josie stopped again. "You really wouldn't have an issue with it?"

"Why in the world would I?"

"Oh, I don't know." She grew serious. "I never imagined feeling like this again. The whole thing has my mind in a jumble."

"Remember when you told me I could talk to you about anything? Well, the same goes for you. I am here for you too. Maybe it will help to unjumble some of those things. Have the two of you discussed this?"

"We have some. I think he's as nervous as I am." The smile that followed was a shaky one.

"You two have been through a lot, Aunt Josie. I think this will be good for both of you."

Josie gave Ana a quick hug and went on her way. "I will think on it, Ana."

Once Josie was out of earshot and Jacob was back at her side, Ana let out a giggle. "You would think she was a teenager!"

Jacob laughed too. "I agree, though. They do make a great couple."

"Yes, they do."

"Would you like to go for a walk? It's such a beautiful afternoon." He looked hopeful.

"Sure, I guess I could go for a short one. I will need to be back soon to help Josie with supper, though."

"All right, a short walk it is."

They walked in silence as they headed around the front of the house and toward the lavender meadow. Ana wondered how much longer she was going to be able to enjoy all those fragrant purple flowers.

She decided now would be the perfect time to gather a big bouquet to take back to the house to dry. That way, she would be able to enjoy their wonderful fragrance throughout the winter months.

Ana had gathered a large bundle before she realized Jacob was standing there watching her. "Oh, I'm sorry. I got carried away and wasn't paying you any attention."

Ana brushed a strand of curls, which had fallen loose in the breeze, behind her ear and stood there waiting for him to speak.

"You are so beautiful."

"Ex…cuse me?" Ana was not sure she had heard him correctly.

"I said, you are so beautiful," he clarified himself as he walked slowly toward her.

"Thank you." Ana was suddenly very weak and was sure she would crumble to the ground at any moment.

Jacob stopped directly in front of her and took her by the hand. "Sit with me for a minute."

Ana sat in complete silence and waited to hear what Jacob had to say next. "I wasn't going to say anything this visit. Now I know I have to."

Ana waited breathlessly.

"Ana, when we were on the train together…well, it's just that I've grown…" He hung his head, obviously frustrated with himself.

After a moment, he took both of Ana's hands in his and looked straight into her eyes. "I have feelings for you, Ana."

"Feelings?" Her naive mind needed clarification.

"Yes, Ana…feelings."

When he looked at her, what she saw in his eyes left no need for further explanation.

"Oh my."

"I felt it first on the train and then more strongly when I read your letter. When I saw you here for the first time, I knew in my heart what I was feeling was real."

Jacob sat for a second waiting for Ana to speak, and when she did not, he went on, "I understand if you don't feel the same way, but I suddenly realized I couldn't leave without telling you how I feel." He finished by releasing her hands and dropping his head. Ana realized by Jacob's forlorn look that he had misunderstood her silence.

"Oh, Jacob," Ana began, hoping that she could fix things, "I'm sorry, but I feel you have read my reaction all wrong. I was not expecting this. But I do welcome it."

He raised his eyes to meet hers once again, and slowly a sweet smile began to spread across his handsome face. "You do…really?"

"Yes, I do."

He reclaimed her hands, and they sat there, each wanting to hold on to the moment for as long as they could. The breeze kicked up, sending loose curls swirling around Ana's face. Jacob reached out and brushed the strands away, his fingertips lingering gently on her cheek.

"As I said before, you are beautiful!"

They talked a while longer until Ana realized how late it was getting. She really needed to get back to help Josie with supper, so they promised to continue their talk later. The couple stood, and Ana gathered her bundle of lavender before they began their walk back to the house.

Josie, however, had other plans for their evening. She informed Ana of her idea to have a big birthday celebration for her the following day. She planned to include everyone from the ranch. Therefore, they spent the rest of the evening preparing for the event. Jacob and Ana's talk would have to wait.

14

September 9, 1863
Do I smell smoke?

THE THOUGHT CAUSED Ana to sit straight up in bed and glance around the room, looking for the source. She heard a commotion outside and raced to the window where she saw Ben and Hank, two of the ranch hands, nursing a fire under a large spit. On that spit was one of the largest pigs Ana had ever seen.

She stood watching in amazement until Lucy came running into the room.

"Happy birthday, Ana!" Lucy threw her arms around her sister in a monstrous hug, knocking her off-balance.

"Thank you, Lucy!"

"Did you see the pig?"

"I did!"

"Aunt Josie is downstairs making a special breakfast for you. You should get ready and come on down."

"I will." They gave each other another quick hug, and then Lucy was out the door.

"Seventeen!" Ana marveled. "But more importantly," Ana continued as she stared at her reflection in the full-length mirror, "Jacob has feelings for me!"

She wrapped her arms around herself and spun around in a circle. "It is going to be a glorious day!"

It was glorious indeed! The whole ranch came alive with music, food, and fun! It was absolutely the best birthday ever! The only thing that would have made it better was if Ana's father could have been there. She so hoped he was doing well.

Thankfully, Ana didn't have much time to dwell on her father's absence. There was too much to do and too many people to keep her occupied. When she didn't think there could possibly be more, Josie announced it was time for presents.

"This one is from all of us ranch hands," Hank announced as he handed the birthday girl a small package.

Inside was a small leather pouch with Ana's initials branded onto the side.

"Here, you wear it like this." He took it from her, putting the strap around her neck, and then put one arm through it, causing it to angle across her body and hang down at the side. "There!" he proclaimed proudly.

"Thank you all so much! I love it!" It was such a lovely and practical gift.

"Here, this is from Joe and me," Sarah told Ana.

"Oh, how lovely!"

Their gift was a handwoven blanket, typical of their Indian heritage, with rich earth-tone colors zigzagging across the piece from top to bottom.

Next was a beautiful blue cotton blouse with beaded accents Beth announced she had made after returning from shopping the previous morning.

"How in the world did you find the time?" Ana knew Beth had her hands full with an adventurous Isaiah.

"Sarah helped with Isaiah, or it would have been impossible."

Thomas and Lucy gave her an assortment of hair ribbons and a new brush and mirror. A surprise gift from her father revealed a hair comb trimmed in gold. Josie had to outdo everyone, of course. She announced that the mare Noah had broken right after they arrived in Flint Creek was now Ana's!

"You'll have to think of a good name for her," Lucy informed her sister. "She doesn't have one yet."

"I will! I will think of the perfect name."

"Grasshopper comes to mind," Jacob whispered in her ear. Ana was glad no one was paying attention at that moment, for she almost choked on her laughter.

"Come with me," Jacob whispered again.

He took Ana by the hand and led her away from the festivities to the end of the house. He then motioned for her to have a seat in the swing hanging from the oak tree.

"I wanted to give you my gift in private." He then presented her with a small black-velvet pouch.

"You didn't have to get me anything, Jacob," Ana told him as she took the gift from him.

"I wanted to, though."

Inside the pouch was the most beautiful locket she had ever seen! It was gold with an elegant filigree design etched into it and hanging on a delicate long chain.

"Oh, Jacob, you shouldn't have!"

"Go ahead and open it. Josie helped me with the rest."

Ana gave him a puzzled look but did what he asked. Inside was a picture of her mother. Ana recognized it to be from a family photo, made right before she became ill.

"I don't know what to say."

"There is room for one more, but I thought you would like to have one of your mother's in there."

"It's perfect. Thank you, Jacob," Ana said her through tears.

He then took the necklace from her, hooked it around her neck, and let it fall gently into place. "There. Now it's perfect."

"I will treasure this forever!" Ana pressed the pendant gently to her heart.

"You, my precious Ana, are the treasure." Jacob took her free hand and helped her out of the swing.

They stood in silence, enjoying the moment a while longer, the sounds of the party surrounding them. Way too soon, Jacob announced they should get back to the others. Ana noticed Josie watching them as they rejoined the group.

Ana mouthed a quiet, "Thank you," and Josie replied with a tearful smile.

The party went on for the next few hours—plenty of dancing and singing and lots more food. Ana didn't think she had ever had so much fun. The crowd began to go their separate ways, and the party started dying down.

Ana sat on one of the porch swings while clean up was going on since no one would let her help. Lucy had been keeping her company but had fallen asleep with her head on her big sister's shoulder. This was how Jacob found them.

"All tuckered out, huh?" he asked, brushing the hair out of Lucy's face.

"I believe she had more fun than any of us. She definitely exerted the most energy anyway."

"That she did." He took a seat in the closest rocker. "I talked to Noah and Beth and then Josie and Thomas about church tomorrow."

"What did they say?"

"They said they would love to go. I think Noah and Beth agreed more as a going-away present for me, but I will take what I can get."

"That's wonderful," Ana sounded sleepier than she meant to. "I'm looking forward to it."

She really was too. Jacob had mentioned it several times, and Ana could see how passionate he was about it. This caused her to be more curious than she ever dreamed possible.

"Well, for now, I think it's a good idea for us all to get some sleep," Jacob pointed out.

Ana smiled her agreement, and Jacob stood and lifted Lucy in his strong arms. "Lead the way," he said.

Jacob followed Ana up to Lucy's room, and Ana watched as he laid the sleeping child in her bed, covered her up, and then pressed a kiss to her brow.

"Good night, doodlebug," he whispered before he stood and motioned for Ana to lead the way from the room.

They made their way back down the stairs and out to the front porch, stopping to stand face-to-face. He then took Ana's hands in his and placed a kiss on each. "Good night, Ana Grace, and happy birthday."

"Thank you, Jacob, for everything."

"See you in the morning." He then made his way down the porch steps.

Ana made her way back inside to find Josie waiting for her in the sitting room.

"Come, have a seat." Josie patted the space beside her on the love seat.

"Is there something wrong, Aunt Josie?"

"No, nothing wrong. I just feel that it is my duty to talk to you about you and Jacob."

"You don't approve." Ana was crushed. "I felt sure you would."

"Oh, honey, I do—honestly! You're just so young, and well, your father is not here, or your mother, or Liza."

Ana suddenly understood what Josie was trying to do, so she sat there patiently waiting for her aunt to find the words.

Josie shook her head. "I am dreadful at this."

Ana reached and took her by the hand. This seemed to give Josie courage, and she was able to continue. "I can tell you and Jacob are having some serious feelings for each other. I want to make sure you know everything you need to know. Not that I know everything myself."

"Josie, Liza had that talk with me several years ago, so there is really no need for you to worry about it."

The flood of relief on Josie's face was almost comical.

"Well, all right then," she said in a slight rush. "There is more to relationships besides that, though. So I want to make sure you know that if you have any questions, you can come to me."

"I know I can, Josie. And I appreciate it so much. There *are* some questions I have—well, one in particular, but I don't know if *anyone* can help me with it."

"Try me."

"What am I going to do when he leaves tomorrow? What if I never see him again?" Ana began to cry.

She had been meditating privately on these questions all day and couldn't hold back the emotions they brought any longer.

"Oh, honey, everything will be fine, you will see." Josie wrapped her arms around Ana's shoulders.

"But he is going back to that awful war! You didn't see the things I did before we left Chattanooga, Aunt Josie! People were dying! He could die too!"

"From what I have seen and heard from your Jacob, he is a very capable young man. This means he is just as capable of a soldier. He will be fine."

"Oh, I hope so, Aunt Josie! I don't know what I would do if something were to happen to him."

"You will have to give all your worry over to God, Ana. Let Him take care of Jacob for you."

"You talk to God, Josie?"

"Yes, Ana, I do. As often as I can."

"I didn't know."

"Well, I knew your father's aversion to the subject, and I was afraid you may feel the same way. It was truly wrong for me not to share my beliefs, and I am very ashamed."

"Do you go to church, or should I say did you, before we came?"

"Yes, every Sunday. It's going to feel good to go back tomorrow morning."

"I am so sorry we have been keeping you from church. I just feel awful."

"No worries, my dear. How do you believe, Ana?"

"I'm really new at this. We attended church before Mama died, but not since. Liza tried to keep on teaching us. However, when Papa found out, he became furious. She never tried after that. Didn't even mention it—at least not until we were getting ready to leave Chattanooga. She had Lucy and me to pray with her. Then on the train, Jacob talked to me about God and about praying to Him. I have been trying to ever since."

"Jacob talked to Thomas and me about it for a while this morning. He is a real, strong believer. It makes me feel good to now know he has talked to you about it as well."

Ana smiled and then yawned. "There is still so much that I don't understand, Josie."

"Just keep seeking. God will work it all out for you. And never forget you can come to me anytime. For now, I think we need to head on to bed. We have another busy day tomorrow."

Ana gave Josie a hug. "Thank you, Aunt Josie."

"You are most welcome, my sweet Ana. You know your mother would be so proud of you."

After a kiss to Ana's forehead, they said their good-nights, putting an end to a very special day.

15

"To be able to enjoy the reward of a heavenly home, we have to be saved by the wonderful grace of our Lord and Savior, Jesus Christ. The Lord makes his plan of salvation very clear and very easy to understand.

"Turn your Bibles to St. John, chapter 5 and verse 24. Jesus says in this verse. 'Verily, verily, I say unto you, he that heareth my word, and believeth on him that sent me, hath everlasting life, and shall not come into condemnation; but is passed from death unto life.'

"He is telling us here, all we have to do is believe. By believing and accepting Him, it is possible for us to have life everlasting. Now turn with me to First John and read with me the next step. Chapter 1 verse 9 tells us, 'If we confess our sins, he is faithful and just to forgive us our sins, and to cleanse us from all unrighteousness.'

"We all sin on a daily basis, but it is up to us to confess those sins with a contrite heart. The Lord has promised when we do this, that He will show us forgiveness. We are not done there. Turn to Romans chapter 10 and look at verse 9. 'That if thou shalt confess with thy mouth the Lord Jesus, and shalt believe in thine heart that God hath raised him from the dead, thou shalt be saved.'

"He is referring here, of course, to the great resurrection of Jesus on the third day. How wonderful to know how easy it is to receive salvation and the promise of a heavenly home. Now, folks, I do not know your hearts, but there could be someone here today who has yet to follow His plan of salvation and accept Him as their Lord and Savior, someone here who has yet to stake claim to their eternal home in heaven. I pray that if you are that person, if you have not taken the steps I have read to you here today, you will before it is too late."

"It's so good to see you back this morning," Pastor Scott told Josie as they made their way out of the morning service.

He was probably in his mid-sixties and a small-statured man. However, he carried himself as though he were seven feet tall. The thin rim of hair, which encircled his head, was snowy white. And he wore tiny gold-rimmed glasses, which framed his elvish face.

"It is good to be back. I would love for you to meet my nieces," she told him as she shook his hand. "This is Lucy."

"Hello, Lucy. It's a pleasure to meet you," the pastor greeted Lucy.

"Hello," Lucy returned.

"And this is Ana Grace," Josie added.

"Ana Grace, you look so much like your Mother," Pastor Scott commented. Ana gave him a confused look, and he went on, "Josie has shown me pictures of your mother when I visited the ranch."

Ana nodded in understanding. "It's very nice to meet you, Pastor Scott."

"I hope this is the first of many visits you and Lucy make to our church."

"It *is* the first of many, I assure you. I very much enjoyed it," Anna replied.

Ana really did, even though she seemed to have even more questions than she ever dreamed possible.

"I am so glad to hear it, Ana. Josie, where is this Thomas I have heard so much about?"

"He's on his way out."

They all looked in time to see Thomas walking out of the church, followed by Jacob, Noah, Beth, and baby Isaiah.

"Oh, and there is that young soldier boy, Dalton. Jacob Dalton, I believe," Pastor Scott pointed out.

"Yes, he's the one who rescued Ana and Lucy from the fighting in Chattanooga," Josie informed him.

"I had the privilege of talking at length with him about his adventures and his belief in Christ on the morning before he left for your ranch."

"He told me about meeting you."

"That's Noah, the assistant manager at the ranch, is it not?"

"It is, and his wife, Beth, and their son, Isaiah."

The group stood a few more minutes making small talk before Pastor Scott moved on to greet others exiting the church. Noah and Beth needed to get a fussy Isaiah home for a nap, so they said their good-byes as well. The rest of the group had plans to spend the remainder of the day in town with Jacob as he was to be leaving later in the afternoon.

They began with a wonderful lunch at the hotel and afterward strolled around town, taking in the sights. When Lucy discovered the general store was actually open, she begged to go inside.

Ana and Jacob decided to forego the store visit. Instead, they walked to a small courtyard beside the church and took a seat under a large maple tree.

"Ana, you have looked troubled ever since we left the church. Is there something you would like to discuss?"

"Yes, I guess there is. Something Pastor Scott was saying in his sermon worries me."

"What exactly did he say that worries you?"

"Well, if I understood him correctly, a person has to be saved to be able to make it to heaven. Is that right?"

"Yes. That's right."

"To be saved, I have to do the things he said. I have to believe all those things."

"Yes. However, it is not only the believing. The Bible says even the devil believes. To be saved by grace, you have to believe all those things then wait for the call from God to be saved."

"I don't understand."

"You have to be invited by a convicting spirit, and then the Lord will hear your plea and come into your heart." He sensed Ana's confusion and went on, "The Lord tells us, and I am paraphrasing here, our heart is like a door. When the Lord knows you are ready to hear Him and accept Him, He will knock on that door. It's as if your heart starts pounding, and you know beyond a shadow of a doubt that it's Him. You can feel Him leading you to invite Him in so He can save your soul. When He starts knocking, you realize your soul is lost. And if you don't listen to Him, you will die and go to hell."

"You're sure I will know?"

"Yes, Ana. There'll be no doubt."

"I have had that feeling before, but I didn't feel like I needed to be saved. I felt as though I was only supposed to pray."

"Well, that is probably all He wanted from you during those times. He knows you really didn't grow up in the Word, and you needed to learn more. I have no worries for you, Ana. You have been seeking with an open heart. He will save you someday."

"You really believe that, Jacob?"

"Yes, with all my heart. Don't let yourself get discouraged. He works in His own time, not ours. Keep praying and seeking Him. Read in His Word as often as you can and wait on Him. I know you would be welcome here at church. Pastor Scott is a good man, and I trust God will use him to tell you the things you need to hear the most."

"Thank you, Jacob. You don't know how much your words have helped me."

"You're welcome. I'll be praying for you, Ana. You have to promise me again that you'll write to me often and keep me updated."

"I promise," Ana choked up.

Jacob reached and took her hand as the first tear slid down her cheek. His eyes never left hers. With his free hand, he wiped the wayward tear from her face. They then sat in silence for the next few minutes, neither one wanting to voice what was to come in such a short while.

"Hey, there they are!"

Lucy's announcement broke the spell, causing Jacob to release Ana's hand.

"I really hate to tell you, Jacob, but the stage is pulling into town as we speak," Thomas informed him.

Jacob let out a huge sigh. "All right, thank you. I guess it's time then."

"I'm going to miss you, Jacob!" Lucy crawled onto his lap and threw her arms around his neck.

"I'm going to miss you too, doodlebug. You'll have to send me a letter when Ana does, all right?"

"I sure will!" Lucy gave him another quick squeeze and hopped down.

Jacob then stood, turned to Ana, and waited for her to rise as well.

Ana knew this was going to be hard. However, she also knew there was nothing she could do to stop him from leaving. He had a duty to his country to fulfill. Growing up around the military, Ana knew that had to come first. Therefore, taking a deep breath, she stood and began to follow the others toward the depot where she would have to say good-bye to her Jacob, possibly forever.

16

September 30, 1863

"DALTON, YOU HAVE a letter." The corporal tossed the missive into Jacob's lap.

"Thank you," Jacob told him as he walked away.

Jacob looked at the delicate penmanship on the front and knew instantly from whom it came. He stood and headed for the privacy of his tent. His heart began to pound as he started opening the letter, confirming how much he was missing the one who had written it.

> September 21, 1863
>
> Jacob,
>
> Thank you for the word on your arrival in Chattanooga and that all was well with you and my father. It really meant a lot. I hope this letter finds you both still the same.

Things here are going well. School is keeping me busy, however. I did not realize what I was getting myself into, agreeing to finish before Christmas. And we are only a week into the semester! I know it will all be worth it in the end.

Lucy is having the time of her life! She has made so many new friends and seems to be fitting right in. She has been working hard this week on every assignment Mrs. Beason has given her. Enclosed you will find a letter from her as well.

I have even made a good friend of my own! Her name is Katie. We are the same age, and she is so much fun. She has such a wonderful personality and has an infectious laugh. We have been spending a lot of time together this past week.

We actually met on the way to school on the first day. She lives on the small farm between Josie's ranch and town. I am sure you remember seeing it. Anyway, she also goes to church, so we will be able to see each other there as well.

I know you will not be surprised to hear this, but Josie and Thomas have come out in the open concerning their feelings for each other! They were, of course, worried what everyone would think. Actually, most said it was about time! They are so giddy you would think they were teenagers!

We attended church again on Sunday, and I cannot wait to go back. Everyone is so nice and goes out of their way to make Lucy and me feel right at home. They also said to tell you hello and that you were in their prayers.

I have been thinking and praying long and hard on what we discussed in those last few moments you were here. I want to be saved, Jacob! I know beyond a shadow of a doubt if I were to die, I would not receive a heavenly home. This truly frightens me! Pray for me, Jacob!

I think of you often and worry about you so! It troubles my heart and mind so much to think about where you are and what you are doing. I will be truly happy when this horrible war is over! Please, Jacob, stay safe!

Praying for you,
Ana Grace

Jacob wiped the tears from his face and, before doing anything else, began to lift Ana up in prayer. He knew in his heart it would not be long before he would receive word she had accepted Jesus Christ as her Lord and Savior. He also knew that was going to be the best news he would ever receive.

When he had finished his prayer, he refolded the letter and tucked it away in his shirt pocket. He then began reading Lucy's letter and found Ana was right. Lucy was enjoying school. She babbled on and on about her assignments and mentioned several children who were her friends. He was so proud she was doing well.

Once he finished reading Lucy's letter, he said a heartfelt prayer for her as well and then dug out his writing implements to begin his replies.

September 30, 1863

My dearest Ana,

I was so happy to receive your letter and hear all was well back there in Texas.

I was also glad to hear you have made a friend. It helps to know you have someone your age in whom you can confide. You will have to introduce us the next time I visit.

I knew you would have your hands full with school. However, you are right. It will definitely be worth it in the end. Is Katie going to finish early as well? If so, I know that would be such a help to you to have someone to help you study.

I knew it would not take long for Josie and Thomas to admit their feelings! Make sure you tell them they are in my prayers!

You will be glad to know, aside from a few small skirmishes, things here are rather quiet.

Your father is doing well. I see him almost every day in some capacity. I spoke to him briefly about us writing to each other, and he said he had no objections. I hope you don't mind, but I didn't want to cross any lines with him where you were concerned. He said to tell you and Lucy he thought of you both always and would write when he could.

You don't know what you did to my heart when I read you wanted the Lord to save you! I have prayed for that so much lately! I know it will happen too! Keep seeking Him and studying in His word. He will let you know when it is time, and you will have no doubts about it. You better let me know as soon as possible when it happens!

It is almost time for me to head out on patrol duty, so I will close now. I hope to hear from you soon!

Jacob

Jacob penned a quick letter to Lucy as well and headed out with both to get them off in the post. Afterward, he readied himself for a long and tiring patrol duty.

He was still with the regiment under General Bragg's leadership. Even though the Union had control of a large portion of Chattanooga, Bragg's troops had control of Lookout Mountain and the best supply routes. Bragg was hoping to starve out the Union troops by remaining in control of those routes, leaving them pretty much at a standstill.

"So...this is the first time I have really gotten to talk to you since you got back," Caleb Johnson, Jacob's friend and fellow soldier, began. "Where was it you went off to anyway? All anybody would say if we asked was it was official and top secret."

When Jacob did not answer, Caleb went on, "I know you were assigned to getting Colonel Lawson's family out of the city, but you were back for a few days and then gone again."

They had been best friends their whole life, so Jacob knew he had been worried. Jacob also knew Caleb wasn't going to let it rest and decided to tell him the truth. Taking a deep breath, he began to fill his friend in on the events of the past several weeks. He, however, left out his feelings for Ana. He was not ready to share that with him yet.

"Wow!" Caleb said when the story was finished. "Sounds like quite an adventure!"

"Yes. I'm extremely thankful it turned out well."

"So this Ana Grace, how old did you say she was?"

Jacob knew exactly where this was going but answered anyway. "She just turned seventeen."

"Seventeen, huh? Is she a looker?"

"Caleb, don't start," Jacob calmly told his friend.

Caleb knew him well enough and backed off. He also knew Jacob's reaction meant there was something more to the story and gave his friend a small smile to show he was on to him. Jacob shook his head and went back to looking out across the valley below to watch for any movement of the Union troops.

They spent the rest of their patrol time reliving old times and making plans for the future. Caleb could not help but notice that many of Jacob's plans included a place called Hill Country.

October 10, 1863

Ana finished reading Jacob's letter, refolded it, and promised herself she would write back as soon as she returned from Katie's house. They were planning to study all afternoon for the big test they both had coming up on Friday, and she was already running late.

Ana rushed out of the house as fast as she could toward the stable. She threw up a quick wave to Josie and Lucy, who were working near the chicken coop. She said a prayer as she saddled Star, thanking God that Jacob and her father were safe. At least they were a few days ago anyway. She also prayed Jacob was right, that God would soon save her.

"I'm sorry, Katie! I can't seem to concentrate this afternoon!" Ana told her friend when she had asked the same question for the third time.

"You do seem preoccupied. Is everything all right?"

"Yes, everything is fine. I just have so much on my mind lately."

"Have you heard anything?" Katie knew Ana had been worried about her father and Jacob.

"Yes, actually. I received a letter from Jacob today. That's why I was late getting here. I couldn't leave without reading it first."

"How are things with him and your father then?"

"He and Father are well. Jacob said things were somewhat quiet right now. The Yankees have control of part of the city, but the South still maintains control of Lookout Mountain and all the best supply lines."

"Well, that's good news at least."

"Yes. I know it will not stay quiet for long. The Yankees want Chattanooga, and I believe they will stop at nothing to get it. It makes me worry about my neighbors and friends."

"Oh, Ana, I am sure they're fine. Surely Jacob or your father would have told you otherwise."

"I guess I need to just hand it over to God and let Him do His job. I have to trust in Him to take care of them."

"That's all you can do, Ana. There's no sense in making yourself sick with worry over something completely out of your control."

"I know you're right."

The room fell silent for a short time.

"Is there something else you are not telling me?" Katie sensed there was more to her friend's distracted mood.

They had been friends for such a short time, but Katie could already read her like an open book. Ana had not discussed this with her new friend yet, but she now knew it was time. She took a deep breath and began, "I have never been saved, Katie."

The look of understanding on Katie's face took Ana by surprise.

"I kind of expected that. I mean, you told me you only recently started seeking and learning," Katie explained. "I am so sorry! Some witness for Him, I've been! I should've already questioned you, but I didn't want to push you away."

Katie dropped her head in shame.

"Oh no, don't worry about it. It's all right."

"No, I really need to work harder at being bolder where the Lord is concerned. You know you can talk to me about anything, right, Ana?"

"Yes, I know that. I should've already said something. I've talked to Jacob about it some, and he has been very helpful. I'm so frightened the Lord will not want me and never call me to be saved."

"Nonsense. The Lord will most definitely want you, Ana Grace! You have to trust in Him and be patient. He works in His own time."

"That's what Jacob told me. I want to be saved. I want it so badly. There's no doubt in my mind that Mother and Liza are both in heaven right now. I want to be able to see them again someday." The tears were flowing freely now. "I know I am a sinner! I am afraid He won't accept me into His family!"

"Ana, the Bible tells us. 'We all have sinned and came short of the glory of the Lord.' You don't hold the market on sin. It's something we all have to deal with on a daily basis. First John tells us, 'If we confess those sins, that he will forgive us and cleanse us from all unrighteousness.' It says in Romans, 'Everyone who calls on the name of the Lord will be saved.' Does that sound to you like He picks and chooses whom He will save?"

"No."

"Well then, all you have to do, my sweet friend, is believe and accept Him at His word. When your heart is ready, call on His name and ask Him to save you. You know I am here for you whenever you need me."

"Now. Can you pray with m-me now?"

"Oh, yes, Ana!"

The two girls knelt beside the bed in Katie's room, and Ana began to cry out to the Lord as she never had before. She could hear Katie praying also. Then, out of nowhere, the sweetest, calmest feeling washed over her, and all she could do was laugh. It started softly and grew into a loud, exuberant roar! The Lord had saved her soul!

"He saved you didn't He, Ana?" Katie asked through her own jubilation.

"Yes, Katie! Oh yes! He certainly did!"

With that, they embraced, celebrating Ana's victory. The studying was over for the day!

Ana gathered up her things and ran to mount Star and head for home. She had to tell everyone, and then she had a letter to write.

17

October 27, 1863

October 10, 1863

Jacob!

It happened! The Lord has saved me! I cannot believe it! Thank you for praying for me and for the witness you were to me. You will never know how much it all helped. I will forgo the details and save them for when we are face-to-face. For now, I simply wanted you to know the Lord forgave me of my sins, and I will be going to heaven to see Mama and my dear sweet Liza! God is so good!

I hope you and Father are doing well. I still have not received correspondence from him. Therefore, I know he must be busy. I thank you for your taking time to write to me. You are the only link I have, and without a word from you, I feel I would go insane.

Please tell Father that Lucy and I miss him and wish him well. We also pray for him daily. However, I do not think he would welcome that information. I pray someday that will change.

Please continue to pray for me, for I still have so much to learn.

Hope to hear from you soon!

Your sister in Christ,
Ana

"Thank you, sweet Heavenly Father!" Jacob cried tears of joy. "I knew it wouldn't be long, Lord! Thank you so much for saving Ana! Be with her, Lord Jesus and strengthen her each and every day. Watch over her and help her to have the courage to face whatever the devil tries to throw in her path.

"She is young in her belief and I know the devil will try hard to cause her to stumble. Protect her from him, Lord Jesus. Help her to be a light to those around her and help her to lead others to you. All these things I ask in Jesus's sweet name, amen." Jacob rose from his knees and wiped his eyes.

His time in praise to the Lord came to an abrupt halt at the sound of gunfire and shelling making its way up from the valley. Jacob raced toward the edge of the cliff to survey the action below, but stopped when he realized Caleb was running toward him.

"It looks like the Yankees are going to take Browns Ferry! Lawson is about to call for everyone to be on guard in case they try to start up the side of the mountain! They are starting to reinforce the line facing the western slope."

"What about the eastern slope? There should be men watching that side too. The fighting at the ferry could be a diversion."

"Lawson is sending a small battalion over that way just in case."

The last couple of weeks there had been a division in General Bragg's regiment. Ana's father received a promotion to major general and was put in charge of the troops atop Lookout Mountain. Jacob was thankful he was able to stay with him and not have to follow Bragg to Missionary Ridge. Bragg's mistreatment of his men was notorious while Lawson did what he could to take care of his.

Jacob and Caleb began to make their way from Point Lookout to the western side of the mountain where the majority of the troops were. They both looked toward the valley from where the noise emanated once they arrived at the edge. The early morning fog hung thick over the river, blocking any real view of the action below. It was still dark enough, however, to see the occasional flash from soldier's rifles.

They listened over the next several hours as quietness settled back over the valley. It became clear the Union troops had been victorious as the fog lifted to allow sunlight to wash over the land below. After a short time, they began to see Union reinforcements making their way down the river.

The troops began to build a floating bridge across the water, completing it by noon that day. This made it possible for troops to bring supplies into Chattanooga to aid the starving Union forces.

Everyone in Jacob's company knew their peaceful existence high atop the mountain would soon be over. Each of them knew they were in for a fight. They just didn't know when.

November 10, 1863

November 1, 1863

Sweet Ana,

I am sorry it has taken so long for me to respond. Things have been busy around here as of late.

You don't know how happy I was to hear your news! I knew it wouldn't be long, for I felt in my heart that you were ready to receive Christ. I know a great weight lifted from your shoulders, knowing you will be able to spend eternity with your mother and Liza.

Keep praying and studying as much as you can. You are young in your walk with Christ; therefore, the devil will try to trip you up even more than he did before. Hold strong! I will be praying for you and looking forward to hearing the whole story!

As I said earlier, things have been busy. There has been an upheaval within our regimen, putting your father, now a major general, in charge of our particular unit. We are currently holding fast to Lookout Mountain from the vantage point of Craven House.

The Union troops are still in the city and have recently overtaken Browns Ferry. Meaning, they will be able to get more supplies into the city and be able to strengthen their defenses. We feel confident, however, we will be able to maintain control of the mountain.

Please keep us all in your prayers, and I will do the same for you. I am looking forward to hearing from you again soon.

Your brother in Christ,
Jacob

P.S. Here is a list of scriptures for you. There are so much more I could put down, but we will start with these: Psalms 143:10, Romans 12:1–2, 2 Peter 1:5–8.

"Is that letter from Jacob?" Josie asked when she entered the sitting room.

Ana had picked the letter up from the post office on her way home from school and had just finished reading it for the second time when Josie came in.

"Yes, it is."

"It has been a few weeks since you received a letter, has it not? Is everything all right?" Josie made her way to sit beside her niece on the setee.

"Yes, Jacob and Father are fine. Father is now in charge of Jacob's regiment, and they are currently trying to maintain control of Lookout Mountain. I am so worried about them, Josie!"

"I know you are, my dear," she consoled. "But you will have to trust in the Lord to take care of them. How about we say a quick prayer for them right now?"

"That is a splendid idea."

Ana and Josie bowed their heads and poured their hearts out to the Lord. Ana felt somewhat better once finished but still had a nagging uneasiness deep inside.

"The meal was wonderful, Josie! You really outdid yourself!" Thomas said a bit too enthusiastically as he took his empty plate to the kitchen.

"Why, thank you, Thomas!" Josie mirrored Thomas's emotion as she followed him from the room.

The rest of the dining room occupants began to giggle as soon as they were out of sight.

"They are so funny!" Beth announced.

"You should see how they are if they think no one is watching! They are so giddy and so…silly," Ana informed everyone.

"Well, I think it is wonderful!" Sarah interjected.

"Don't get me wrong, Sarah. I think it's wonderful too! In fact, I cannot wait until—"

The lovebirds chose that moment to make their way back into the dining room. Everyone couldn't help but notice the conspiring looks on their faces.

"We have an announcement to make," Josie informed them.

Josie looked to Thomas, and he took a deep breath and began to speak, "I have asked Josie for her hand in marriage." He finished the statement with a huge smile.

"What does that mean?" Lucy asked innocently.

"Thomas and Josie are going to get married," Ana explained to her little sister.

Lucy let out a squeal of delight, causing the whole room to erupt in cheers, including baby Isaiah.

"Oh, Josie! I am so happy for you!" Ana hurried to embrace her aunt. "Thomas, I knew you were supposed to stay with us for some reason."

"So did I, Miss Ana. So did I."

Everyone took their turn in congratulating the newly engaged couple and then adjourned to the sitting room for coffee and wedding plans.

"So when is the big day?" Joe asked once everyone took a seat.

"Well, we decided to do it the second weekend in December. That way, we will not interfere with Thanksgiving or Christmas," Josie told everyone.

"That will be great! But what about your dress? That doesn't give much time to get one made," Ana voiced her concern.

"Well, I was kind of hoping I could enlist Beth's help with that."

Ana remembered the blouse Beth had made her for her birthday. She had embellished it with very detailed beadwork and all in one night! Therefore, she had no doubts that Beth could get the job done.

"I would be honored to do anything you need me to do, Josie," Beth assured her.

"Oh, thank you, Beth!"

"You can count on me to help too, Josie," Sarah offered.

"I was hoping you would say that."

The men began fidgeting as the discussion continued and found a reason to excuse themselves from the room. They claimed they had plans of their own to make. The women found it all rather amusing.

Later that night, as Lucy and Ana were readying for bed, Josie came into Ana's room.

"Girls, I would like to speak to you for a moment."

"Sure, what is it?" Ana asked her.

"There are two very important jobs I would like to ask you to do for me."

"What jobs, Aunt Josie?" Lucy wanted to know.

"It seems tradition calls for there to be a maid of honor and flower girl standing up with the bride during a wedding. I was hoping I could count on you two to fill those positions for me."

"Aunt Josie, I would love to!" Ana's eyes filled with tears.

"Me too!" Lucy exclaimed.

"I am so happy!" Josie started to cry and laugh at the same time.

Ana rushed to her side and wrapped her arms around her aunt in a tight embrace. Lucy joined in, and they stood relishing the moment as long as they could.

"It's getting late, girls," Josie announced. "We can continue all of this tomorrow." She gave them both another quick hug and then headed out of the room.

"I get to be a flower girl!" Lucy was so excited.

"I know, and that's a really big job too."

"I know it is! I am going to be the best flower girl ever!"

"You sure will!" Ana agreed with her and gave her a hug before sending her off to bed.

Ana was not ready to sleep, though. She sat at her desk and took out some paper and readied her pen and ink. She simply had to share this news with Jacob.

18

November 23, 1863

November 10, 1863

Dear Jacob,

I received your letter, and I am thrilled that you and Father are doing well. I am also glad you are together. Please give him my love when you are finished reading this. Also, please share the news that I am about to share with you.

Josie and Thomas announced their engagement! I knew once they admitted their feelings it wouldn't take long for this to happen. They are so suited for each other, and I am so happy for them both.

They have set the date for December 12. I wish it were possible for you and Father to be here to join in the celebration. Please know we all will miss you both.

I have good news of my own! I will finish school on December 18! I think I may try to find some type of work in town afterward, maybe at the mercantile or the dress shop. We will see.

Thank you for the Bible verses. Things have been a little crazy this afternoon, and I have not had a chance to look at them. Keep praying for me, Jacob, and I shall do the same for you.

The hour is late, so I must close for now. Hope to hear from you soon.

Until next time,
Ana Grace

"GENERAL LAWSON, SIR, could I possibly have a moment?" Jacob asked as he approached the man.

"Yes, of course, Dalton." James turned away from his maps and headed toward Jacob.

Together they walked out to the front porch of Craven House in an attempt to find a little privacy.

"Is this a personal matter or business?"

"Personal matter, sir. I received a letter from Ana, and she asked me to let you know Ms. Keller and Thomas Snider have announced their engagement. They are to wed December 12."

"Oh, that is news! Josie has lived alone for a long time, and Thomas is a good man. Please let them know I wish them the very best."

"I will surely do that. You will also like to know Ana is set to finish school on December 18th. She's worked very hard and is very excited about having her schooling behind her."

"Oh my, that is wonderful! Let her know how proud I am of her."

"You know, sir, and I apologize if I am crossing the line," Jacob began cautiously, "but she would probably appreciate to hear from you personally."

The officer dropped his head. "Yes, you're right. I've let both my girls down with my not keeping in touch. I will make a point to pen a letter this evening. Thank you, Jacob."

"You're welcome, sir."

"I feel I should also spend more time getting to know you better."

"Sir?"

"You have feelings for my Ana. Do you not?"

Jacob took a deep breath. "Yes, sir. I do."

"You're a good man, Jacob. And that's what I want for my daughter. What exactly are your intentions where she is concerned?"

"Honestly, I would like very much for this war to be over so I can go back to Texas to be with her. I have never felt this way for anyone in my life."

"So you love her?"

"Yes, sir, very much."

"Does she know this?"

"She knows."

"And how does she feel about you?"

"She feels the same way. We discussed this on my visit there last month."

"I must admit, this is a little overwhelming. It's hard to think of my Ana as old enough for such things. However, I know she is. Her mother was only seventeen when we wed. It simply is a hard thing for a father to realize his baby girl is all grown up."

"I'm sure it is. Please, let me assure you, my intentions for Ana are honorable. Even if the war was over today and I could head back to her, I know she is not ready for marriage. I know I would have to give her time and take things slowly."

"That's good to hear. Know that you have my blessing."

"Thank you, sir."

The two men shook hands, and the general made his way back inside the house. Jacob stood for a moment in shock at what had transpired over the past few minutes. Nevertheless, he also knew enough to send up a prayer of thanks that it had.

"Hey, Jacob. What are you up to? Kissing up to the boss man? Or should I say, to the future father-in-law?" Caleb teased as he made his way to Jacob's side. "Oh, wait a minute. The boss man *is* the future father-in-law!"

"Stop it, Caleb!" Jacob gave a little punch to Caleb's gut.

"Ugh! Don't beat me up me for telling the truth!"

"I think I'll just beat you up for the fun of it! What are you doing anyway?"

"Looking for you. Cook is about to ring the dinner bell. You want to be first in line, don't you?"

"Yes. I'm starving!"

The two men headed around the back of the house and toward the kitchen door. They arrived just in time for the call.

"Soup's on, boys!" the cook yelled from behind the makeshift serving table, causing a stampede of men to head that way.

They had been rationing a good bit the last couple of weeks. Therefore, when there was food, everyone ate their fill.

Jacob and Caleb got their plates full and headed to claim a spot beside the campfire. No one said a word for the next few minutes. The only sounds heard were the crackle of the campfire and the scrape of forks on tin plates.

"That was actually pretty good," Caleb said as he finished off his stew.

"Yes, it was," Jacob agreed. "I could go for another plateful."

"Me too!" Caleb laughed. "Too bad cook said no seconds!"

"Yep!"

"So what were you talking to General Lawson about earlier?"

"I was telling him about the letter I received from Ana this afternoon."

"What about it?"

This caused Jacob to laugh because he knew his friend wasn't going to give up without some details. "Well, if you must know…"

"Yep, I must!"

Jacob laughed harder, and Caleb joined in.

"Seriously, Ana's Aunt Josie and Thomas Snider, the train conductor I told you about"—Caleb nodded in understanding, and Jacob went on—"have announced their engagement. Ana wanted me to tell her father."

"It looked a little more serious than that," Caleb sounded disappointed.

"Well…," Jacob began, deciding to go ahead and share everything, "he asked me about my feelings for Ana."

"I knew it was more serious! What did you say?"

"I told him the truth. That I am in love with her and plan to go back to Texas as soon as I can and eventually ask her to marry me."

"All that and you're still breathing." Caleb chuckled at his own joke.

"I was a little worried when he started asking questions. But he was actually very accepting of the idea. He asked how she felt about me, and I told him we had confessed our feelings for each other on my visit down there."

"Wow! Does he know everything? I mean, about her going to church and being saved and all?"

"No, Ana doesn't think he would be too receptive to that information right now."

"You definitely don't want to push the man, that's for sure. Baby steps will be best."

"I agree. I pray he is ready to hear his daughter has chosen to follow Christ soon. It would make things so much easier for Ana to have his support."

"I'll be praying for 'em."

"I appreciate it, my friend!"

The night ended with patrol duty for both men. They always managed to luck out and get to be on patrol together, so neither minded too much. However, even though they were together, it still was destined to be a long night.

19

JACOB AND CALEB watched as a heavy fog blanketed the entire mountain range and settled on the vast valley below. Even though the denseness created the illusion of sitting atop the clouds, it also filled the air with eeriness that neither Jacob nor Caleb could dismiss. They finished patrol around two in the morning and headed back to camp. Luckily, they were able to sleep until around sunup. They ate breakfast after waking and spent the next several hours cleaning their guns and campsite.

Everyone's mood was light despite the heavy fog that still hung in the air. The fog made it impossible to see more than twenty feet into the woods behind the house or in front down the mountainside.

"Hey, Jacob, is that you?" Caleb asked as Jacob's figure began to appear in front of him through the murkiness.

"Yes. It's me."

"This fog is something else, ain't it?"

"I don't think I have ever seen it this bad."

"Me either. What's on the agenda for the rest of the day?" Caleb sat down and leaned back against a fallen tree.

"General Lawson said he wanted to beef up patrols a bit since the fog was so thick. But since we pulled a long night, we are exempt until later today."

"That's good. In that case, I might try to get a in few extra winks." Caleb laid his head back and covered his face with his hat.

"Sounds like a good idea to me. I think I'll try to write Ana first."

No sooner had he gotten out pen and paper and sat down than it began. Shots rang out, and soldiers began scrambling for their lives.

"What's happening?" Caleb asked as he rolled over and grabbed his rifle, still half dazed from sleep.

Jacob was already ducking behind a tree with his rifle in hand.

"Yankees!"

Jacob rolled to his stomach and, using the tree as a shield, began firing through the fog at the blue coats as they magically appeared before him.

"I just *thought* this was going to be a boring day!" Caleb said, dodging a shot. He quickly rolled over into position, threw his rifle over the top of the tree trunk he had been leaning against, and began firing right along with Jacob.

It was total chaos for the next several hours. Men were screaming, running, shooting, and being shot. The ground began to grow cluttered with gray and blue.

Jacob took every opportunity to scan the area for General Lawson but was never able to see him. Thankfully, he and Caleb were able to stay together throughout the fighting.

Jacob prayed whenever he was able to take a moment to do so. *Dear Lord, please help us out of this!*

Jacob and Caleb did what they could to help their fallen comrades in the midst of the fighting. They would pull them to safety, shield them from further attack, or gather personal effects from the ones who didn't make it. It was by far the worst battle either of them had ever seen.

Jacob would scan the scene in search of Ana's father every chance he got. He made out several of the other officers but never laid eyes on the general. He continued to pray. Ana could not lose her father too.

The battle had been raging for hours, and the sun was fading in the western sky when Jacob made his way to the storage shed beside the house. Caleb came crashing down beside him just as bullets struck the side of the building above their heads, sending splinters of wood showering down over them.

"This ain't looking too good, Jacob!" Caleb said in a breathless rush.

"No, no, it ain't. Have you caught a glimpse of Lawson during all of this?"

"No." Caleb ducked another shot. "I'm sure he's fine. We'll find him."

"I hope so!" Jacob finished reloading his rifle and moved to fire off a shot.

"Wish we could use those big guns!" Caleb followed his lead and fired a round as well.

"Yeah, this would be a different fight if we could!"

"Yep."

There were two cannons at Craven House, but they were unable to use them for fear of hitting their own men. Therefore, they relied solely on their rifles, sidearms, sabers, and bowie knives.

"I have to get in that house!"

"You're crazy! There's no cover between here and the house!"

"I have to go! I have to make sure he is not in there!"

"You're not going without me!"

"Well, let's go!"

The two men took off running for their lives, somehow managing to reach the house unscathed.

The house was still standing even with all the damage it had received. Thankfully, the Yankees had not taken control of it yet. They made their way through the dimly lit house, taking time to fire out at the enemy whenever they got the chance. They searched the first floor and then made their way up the stairs to search the rooms up there.

They entered one of the bedrooms used by the Confederate troops as a meeting room. There, in a heap on the floor, they found him. Both Jacob and Caleb stopped dead in their tracks, afraid to move—afraid of what they would find. Suddenly they saw movement coming from the injured man.

"General!" Jacob and Caleb rushed to his side.

They found Lawson severely injured. Miraculously, none of the shots appeared in vital areas. His right leg seemed to be where his worst injury was located. Jacob gave it a quick look and could see everything below the knee was virtually unrecognizable.

The men knew he could survive his injuries. They just had to get the bleeding stopped or at least slowed and then get him to safety. He might lose his leg, but he would still be alive. They worked as fast as they could. They tightly covered the wounds and then began the task of trying to move him down the stairs and out of the house.

They had to make it up the side of the mountain to where they were sure the rebels were still in control. Once they reached the back door, Jacob decided he would carry Lawson first, and Caleb would cover them as best as he could.

"Jacob?" Lawson forced out as Jacob hoisted him into the air.

"Yes. Caleb Johnson is with me."

"Yes, sir, we're going to get you out of here." Caleb made ready at the door.

"You should…have…left me," Lawson choked out.

"We couldn't do that, sir! Now hang on. It's going to be a rough one!" Jacob then burst through the door into the fading light. He shot out across the backyard and into the cover of the trees.

Jacob went as fast and as hard as he could up the side of the mountain—as fast as the dead weight on his shoulder would allow anyway. Caleb fired off shots as he chased up the hill after them. Overall, the rescue and retreat went rather smoothly.

They had run into reinforcements four hundred yards into the trees and had a clear path the rest of the way. Jacob and Caleb swapped roles close to the top of the mountain, and Caleb carried Lawson the rest of the way.

They finally made it back to the only road off the mountain, Summerton Road. There they ran into more troops headed to strengthen the line the South was forming to protect Lookout. Commandeering a horse from one of the infantry, they draped the out-cold body of the general across the horse, secured him to the saddle, and then set out at a run. They had to get him to a doctor!

They made their way down the winding mountain road and found a little church alongside Chickamauga Creek the rebels used as a hospital. There, two men who were working with the doctor met them at the edge of the yard. They helped take the general inside and straight to a makeshift table of church pews and wooden planks.

The scene at that little church was a gruesome one. There were wounded men everywhere you looked. Looking out the window, Jacob saw a man carrying an arm and tossing it onto a pile of other removed limbs. He knew Caleb had also seen it by the guttural sound he made.

The smell of blood and death hung thick in the air. It was about all Jacob could do to hold it together. Poor Caleb had to excuse himself from the room.

Jacob watched as his friend walked out of the church and to the creek bank. Caleb made his way as far upstream as he could. He then knelt down and began splashing water on his face.

Jacob returned his attention back to the carnage in front of him when he heard the doctor order Lawson's clothing removed. The doctor came to Jacob's side as the men began the task.

"Who is this gentleman?"

"Major General James Lawson. He was in the battle taking place at Craven House."

"I see. A general, huh?" The doctor searched for a non-blood-soaked spot on his shirttail to wipe the grime from his glasses. "It looks like he got it pretty bad."

"Yes, sir."

"He's lost a lot of blood, and he's gonna lose that leg, but he should be fine. That is, of course, unless infection sets in. That's always a possibility."

"I understand. Please, do all you can for him, Doc."

"Friend of yours?"

"Yes, sir. Where will he go from here?"

"Once we do all we can here, we will move him to the main hospital in town."

"I thought the Union was in control of most of the city?"

"Yes, but funny thing," he began, "put a few bullets in these men, remove a couple of limbs here and there, and they seem to get along fine." He gave a little chuckle, turned, and headed over to begin working on Lawson's wounds.

Jacob stood there for a moment, considering how he felt about the doctor's little joke and decided he didn't care for it at all. He then turned and walked from the building and away from the stench inside it. He took a deep, cleansing breath once he was well away from the smell.

"That was awful!" Caleb said as he made his way to Jacob's side. "Here, I figured you'd need this." He handed Jacob a cold, wet handkerchief and his canteen he had filled with freshwater.

Jacob took full advantage of both. "Thank, you."

"No problem. Now what? What'd the doc say?"

"He said unless infection sets in, he will probably be fine. He will lose his leg, though. They'll do what they can for him here then send him on into town to the main hospital."

"I hate to hear about his leg, but I'm glad he'll be moving soon. Nobody should have to stay for long in that place." Caleb motioned toward the growing chaos up at the church. "What do you want to do?"

"We need to get back up the mountain and do what we can to help out."

"I was afraid you would say that."

With that, the two men headed back up Summerton Road and back to the fight.

20

December 5, 1863

"I CAN'T BELIEVE you already have the dress ready to try on!" Josie exclaimed.

"I hope you like it," Beth said as she took the dress from the basket she was carrying.

"I'm sure I will love it!"

Beth held up the dress, and there was a chorus of *oohs* and *ahhs* in the room from all the witnesses. Josie hugged Beth fiercely and took the dress behind the dressing screen to change. Sarah followed to help.

"Beth, the dress is beautiful!" Ana told her.

"Yes. It truly is!" Katie agreed.

"Thank you!" Beth beamed with pride.

Just then, Josie made her appearance from behind the screen.

"Oh, Beth! It's absolutely perfect! You're simply amazing!" Josie gushed with excitement.

"Oh, now, Josie, it really isn't that big of a deal."

"Oh, yes, ma'am, it is! Thank you so much!"

"You're so very welcome."

Beth walked over to inspect her work and checked to see if she needed to make any adjustments. She found none.

"Like I said, you are amazing," Josie said when Beth finished her inspection. This caused Beth to beam almost as much as Josie. Josie added, "Since there is nothing else to do to my dress, I was wondering if you thought you would have time to make a couple more. Not quite as fancy, mind you. But I have two in my wedding party that could use something special for that day as well." She nodded toward Ana and Lucy. "These, of course, I insist on paying you for making."

"I think I could manage that just fine."

"Josie, you really don't have to do that." Ana knew she and Lucy had plenty of dresses they could wear.

"Nonsense, I want to do it. Consider it my gift to the two of you for agreeing to be in my wedding."

Ana actually had not had a new dress in quite a while, so she allowed herself to get excited with the idea. When Beth finished taking her measurements, they heard Thomas call from the hallway. Josie had changed back into her regular clothes and stepped from behind the curtain.

"Ladies, could you please come out for a moment?"

Thomas had gone into town to pick up his suit from the tailor and do a little shopping at the mercantile.

"He's back awful quick," Josie pointed out.

They all exited the room and found Thomas waiting in the sitting room sporting a very troubled expression. Ana's heart began to pound in her chest, telling her she really did not want to hear what he had to say.

"Thomas, what is it?" Josie asked.

Thomas looked at her, concern showing in his eyes, then looked at Ana. "You received a telegram."

Ana's heart stopped.

"It's your father. He's been wounded."

All Ana could do was stand there in shock, so Josie spoke for her, "Is he all right?"

"The telegram said he has been shot and is in the hospital in Chattanooga."

"Still alive then?" Josie wanted clarification.

"Yes, he is still alive."

Lucy began crying and clinging to Josie's side.

"L-let me see the telegram, p-please, Thomas," Ana was finally able to say.

He reached out and handed her the paper. She took it, walked to a nearby chair, sat down, and started to read.

FAMILY OF GENERAL JAMES LAWSON, FLINT CREEK, TEXAS

WE REGRET TO INFORM YOU THE GENERAL WAS WOUNDED IN BATTLE ON NOVEMBER 25, 1863—*stop*—INJURIES ARE NOT LIFE THREATENING BUT ARE EX-

TENSIVE—*stop*—CURRENTLY IN HOSPITAL
IN CHATTANOOGA—*stop*—WILL KEEP YOU
UPDATED AS OFTEN AS POSSIBLE—*stop*

CARL MARSHALL MD

"I have to go to him," Ana was matter-of-fact with her declaration.

"I don't think that's a very good idea, Ana," Thomas told her. "Reports at the telegraph office are saying the Union has managed to take the city, and the South has been forced into retreat."

"I don't care. He is my father. He needs me!"

"Ana, Thomas is right." Josie made her way to her niece's side. "It is way too dangerous."

"But, Josie!"

"I can't let you go, Ana. If your father knew what you were thinking, he would tell you the same thing, and you know it."

"But what if he…" Ana could not finish the thought and burst into tears instead.

"Pray, Ana! We will all pray for him to be all right!" Katie told her friend as she knelt beside her and took her hands.

Ana nodded in agreement and then motioned for everyone to gather round her. She determined to start praying right then.

It hit her as soon as the prayer was over. "Jacob! What about Jacob? He was with Father on Lookout Mountain! Why has he not tried to contact me?"

"I'm sure Jacob is fine," Beth tried to console her.

"You will hear from him soon, and you will see that he is all right," Katie tried as well.

"Ana, I'm scared!" Lucy cried as she climbed onto her lap.

Ana then realized she had to be strong for her little sister's sake. She had to be the one to reassure her everything was going to be fine. "I'm sorry. I shouldn't have gotten so upset. Everyone is right. Things are going to be fine, you will see! Father's wounds will heal, and we will all see him again. And Jacob will come home to us too."

What Ana had said hit her, and for the life of her, she could not stop her tears. Jacob had to be all right! She had to see him again!

The next ten days were torturous! Ana would have simply gone mad if it hadn't been for being so busy. Thankfully, they were able to get word from her father twice during this time. He let them know his wounds were healing but didn't go into detail as to where and how bad they were.

He informed Ana that Jacob and another soldier had saved his life by rescuing him from the battle. Unfortunately, he had no other information concerning his whereabouts. This troubled her so much! She didn't know how much longer she could go without hearing from him.

Ana did her best to concentrate on her studies—both in school and in the Word—her prayers, and helping Josie get ready for the big day. Ana also spent as much time as possible with Lucy each day, helping to keep her mind busy as well.

Finally Josie and Thomas's big day had arrived! It seemed the whole town turned out for the event. There was so much activity there was no way, thankfully, to think of anything else.

Everyone felt completely worn out by the end of the day. The happy couple had gone into town to spend a couple of nights at the hotel for their honeymoon while an army of ladies from the church had stayed to help Sarah, Beth, and Ana clean up. Lucy had asked to spend the next couple of days with Beth to play with Isaiah, and Katie invited Ana to stay with her.

"I am so happy for Josie and Thomas!" Katie said once they had finished saying their prayers and were climbing into bed that night.

"So am I. They looked so happy today, did they not?"

"Yes, they did."

Ana was quiet for a moment, and Katie spoke, "Are you all right?"

"Yes. I just have a lot on my mind."

"I know, and I'm so sorry about that." Katie rolled over to face her friend. "It's going to be all right, Ana. I can feel it!"

"I hope you're right."

Ana rolled over, closed her eyes, and begged for sleep to come.

On Monday afternoon, when Ana and Lucy got home from school, Josie met them at the door.

"What is it, Josie?" Ana asked. Josie had never done this, so Ana was worried. That is, until Josie broke out in a huge smile.

"What?" she asked her aunt again.

"Come, I have something for you." Josie ushered her into the house and toward the kitchen.

A small gathering of friends greeted Ana as she stepped into the room.

"Surprise!" Everyone yelled in unison.

"What is this?" Ana tried to keep her emotions in check.

"It's to celebrate your finishing school!" Beth told her as she walked to her side for a hug.

"How did you know I passed my test?" Ana asked, for she had only found out herself right before she left school.

"Well, first of all, I had faith that you would pass," Josie began. "And second...," she started then looked at Noah with a teasing grin.

"And second, I kind of snuck up to your school and asked your teacher," Noah confessed.

The room burst into laughter, and the next couple of hours were exactly what Ana needed. It felt so good to have so many people who loved her around.

"I have a gift for you, Ana," Josie informed her after supper and once they were all in the sitting room.

"You didn't have to get me a gift."

Josie didn't seem to listen as she walked over and handed her an envelope. Ana gently tore the paper and pulled out two train tickets to Chattanooga.

"Josie!"

"Thomas and I have discussed this and prayed really hard about it. We can't keep you from going any longer."

"Who's going with me? Who's the second ticket for?"

"Me," Noah spoke up.

Ana was shocked!

"I couldn't let you go alone. Thomas was going to go…," Josie started to explain.

"But since they are newlyweds, Noah and I offered for him to go instead," Beth finished.

Ana looked down at the tickets and saw they were for the day after Christmas.

"What about Lucy?"

"You know Lucy will be fine here," Josie pointed out.

Through her tears, Ana managed a quiet, "Thank you!"

Ana was going to see her father. She was excited and scared to death all at the same time. What was she going to find when she got there?

21

December 29, 1863
Shreveport, Louisiana

ANA AWOKE IN a place she had hoped she would never see again. So many horrible memories surrounded this town. They all came flooding back like a tidal wave as soon as she stepped off the train late last night.

She was scared out of her mind even though she knew the men responsible for Liza's death were not going to be there. Thankfully, Noah recognized this and went out of his way to reassure her everything would be fine.

They made it from the depot to the hotel across the street without incident. Noah had secured them rooms on the second floor, away from any other guests. He searched Ana's room from top to bottom, making sure all was clear, before heading to his own room next door. Even though she appreciated his efforts, she still spent a fitful night.

The light of a new day forced its way through the window. Ana summoned up the courage to climb out of bed, walk to the window, and look out on the town below. Everything was as she remembered—unfortunately. She had hoped there had been some changes since she was here last to help with erasing the memories of that fateful time.

Noah had ordered room service and a bath for her the night before, and Ana knew they would be up with it any time. She had to take care of something before they came. She knelt beside her bed and called out to her Heavenly Father.

"Dear Lord, I thank You, for Your great many blessings. I know You are aware how hard this is for me to be here in this town again. I also know that You are here with me. In addition, I know You will help me through this. I trust in You, dear Lord.

"Help me in the days to come. I have no idea what shape I will find my Father in when I get there, and that scares me. Help me to be strong, dear Lord. Most of all, help me to be a light to him and help him to find his way back to You.

"It has been so long since I have heard from Jacob. I am so worried about him. Please, Lord, be with him wherever he is. Strengthen him and bless him with Your loving spirit. Touch his heart, Lord, and let him know I am praying for him, that I love him, and that I am counting the days until I can see him again. All these things I ask in your sweet name. Amen."

Just then, there was a knock, and Ana opened the door to find room service bringing up her bath. She instructed them where to set things up and waited for them to fill the tub. Once they were gone, she readied for her bath and spent the next little while relaxing in the warm soothing water.

The gentle sounds of wagon wheels on the dirt street below and the jingle of livestock tack created a sort of lullaby. She allowed the melody to flood her mind as the heat from the water began to melt away the tension that had been building since she and Noah boarded the stage in Flint Creek—tension multiplied by a thousand the moment the train began to slow in Shreveport.

Noah had said the night before he would walk her to the sheriff's office today so she could properly thank those responsible for helping Jacob bring Liza's killers to justice. However, it was nearing lunchtime by the time she finished with her bath and dressed for the day. She quickly wrapped herself in her cloak, checked herself in the mirror, and headed for the door. She did not want to delay this any longer.

She took a long cleansing breath as she reached for the doorknob. Then, with a determined stride, she stepped out into the hallway, leaving all trepidation in the room behind her.

"Well, hello there, little lady." The sheriff came to his feet as she stepped into his office. "How might I help you this chilly morning?"

"Good morning, sir. Are you Sheriff Jones?"

"Yes, yes, I am, and you are?"

"My name is Ana Grace Lawson, and this is Noah, a friend of mine. I wanted to come by and thank you and your men for all you did in the apprehension of the Murphy gang."

"It's a pleasure to meet you both," he said as he shook both their hands. "Lawson, huh? You must be that colonel's daughter, the one who was on the train when that slave woman was taken."

"Yes. However, she was not a slave. She was a free woman and one who was very dear to me."

"My apologies, ma'am, for everything. I do remember now that Dalton boy telling me she had cared for you and your sister for many years."

"Yes, sir, she did."

"Tragic what happened to her. I hated it from the moment I heard about it. It was my pleasure in helping to take those hoodlums down. They had been a thorn in my side for way too long, with their stealing and troublemaking. It wasn't until what happened to your Ms. Liza that I had enough evidence to do anything about it. Actually—and I am sure Dalton told you this already—we had gone that night to serve a search warrant. But when Dalton found that shawl…well, that was all the evidence I needed."

"As I said, I appreciate everything. Is there any way I could personally thank the rest of the men involved?"

"Most of them will be pretty hard to track down, but my boy, Seth, was there that night and should be back here any minute."

"He's also your deputy, right?" Ana asked, hoping she had remembered Jacob's story correctly.

"Yes, he is, as a matter of fact. Here he comes now."

Just then, a young man, whom Ana guessed to be the same age as Jacob but much bigger, walked through the door. He was so tall that he had to duck slightly to get inside. In addition, his shoulders were so broad Ana could have sworn she saw him turn sideways a touch to clear the doorjambs.

He noticed Noah first and gave a quick but cordial greeting. Then he met Ana's eyes and seemed to freeze. His reaction took her by surprise. Thankfully, he was able to recover quickly, tipping his hat and finishing with a smile. "Howdy, ma'am." His voice, deep and smooth.

"Hello."

"Seth, this here's Ms. Ana Grace Lawson, the colonel's daughter. You remember from the Murphy gang case?"

"Oh, yes, Ms. Lawson," he began as he held out his hand for the customary handshake. "It's a pleasure to meet you."

"It's a pleasure to meet you as well." Ana allowed him to take her hand in his.

He held it for a moment, studying her eyes and face. Ana felt the heat began to rise in her cheeks. Thankfully, Noah cleared his throat and broke the spell. Seth then released her hand and gave a quick look toward Noah.

"This is Noah," Ana informed Seth when she finally remembered to make the introduction. "He is accompanying me to Chattanooga to visit my father. Father was wounded in battle and is in a hospital there."

"Oh my! I am so sorry to hear about that. Is he going to be all right?" the sheriff asked with genuine concern.

"From what we have been able to find out, yes. However, we have no idea as to the extent of his injuries."

"You do realize the Yankees have control of Chattanooga now?" he wanted to know.

"Yes, we're aware. We have been in close contact with the leaders of the Union troops there, and they have assured our safety. The last we heard, my father was almost well enough to leave the hospital. I am hoping we will be able to take him back to Texas with us."

"Well, we wish you the best, young lady."

"Thank you." Ana then turned her attention back to Seth. "I have already thanked your father. Now I want to thank you for all your help with the Murphy gang."

"Trust me, it was my pleasure. We've had issues with them for years. It felt good to see them get what was coming to them, for all the things they had done around here. But most of all, for what they had done to that poor woman."

"As I said, I thank you."

"You are most welcome." He flashed Ana another look at his brilliant smile. The light finally dawned—he was flirting with her!

"Hey, I tell you what," Sheriff Jones began. "We were about to head over to the hotel for lunch. Why don't the two of you join us—my treat? It's the least I can do after you being so nice as to stop by with a thank-you."

"Really, you don't have to do that," Ana told him.

"Oh, come on. You really should take him up on it. He doesn't come off that wallet of his very often," Seth tried.

"Seriously, I would love to treat the two of you to lunch," the sheriff offered again.

"Well, all right, I suppose," Ana gave in and looked at Noah, who gave a slight shrug of his shoulders.

Both the sheriff and his deputy gave a look of victory and began leading the way out onto the boardwalk and to the hotel.

"So what's your story, Noah? How'd you luck up and get to be on this trip with such a lovely lady?" the sheriff asked as they waited for their food to arrive.

"I help manage the ranch her aunt owns. When this trip was being planned, there was never any doubt that I would go along with her to keep her company"—Noah paused only to give Seth a quick look—"and for her protection."

"That's mighty nice of you." Seth returned the look and added a knowing smile along with it.

Ana felt the tension growing between the two. Sheriff Jones must have also. He broke the mounting silence rather quickly.

"So, Noah, how big a ranch we talkin'?" the sheriff wanted to know.

"Over one hundred thousand acres."

"Over one hundred thousand! Cattle?"

"Yes."

"I bet you can fit a lot of head on that much land."

"Yes, you can."

"She and her husband must have worked really hard for a long time for that."

"Actually, Aunt Josie's husband passed before the ranch ever got that big," Ana informed him. "She has grown her ranch and cattle business on her own for many years now. Well, not all by herself. Noah and his father help keep the place running. It's safe to say she wouldn't have been able to have done it without the two of them."

"I don't know about that," Noah said. "She is pretty resourceful, definitely able to take care of things."

"She sounds like an amazing woman. I may have to ride off down there and introduce myself," Jones teased.

"Her husband would be glad to meet you as well," Ana assured him.

"Oh, I thought you said…" His face flushed with embarrassment.

"She recently remarried."

"Oh, well, seems I am always a day late and a dollar short." Jones gave disappointed chuckle.

"So, Noah," Seth began again, "how about you? You married?"

"Yes, he is. He also has the sweetest, most precious little boy you ever did see. He looks exactly like his father. Well, except for the eyes. Isaiah's eyes are a darker brown, just like his mother's."

Seth's eyes moved from Noah's to Ana's dark-green ones. She suddenly realized she had given Seth the answer he had been looking for. The satisfaction on his face was unmistakable. He had thought she and Noah were a couple.

Noah quickly spoke up, obviously having noticed Seth's revelation, "I wish they would hurry with the food. I'm really getting hungry."

"They are kinda slow here, but the food makes up for it," the sheriff promised.

Seth finally tore his eyes away from Ana's and reached for his drink glass. It was obvious the wheels were turning in his mind, and Ana knew he was planning his next move. Luckily, the waiter came out of the back with their food.

Seth seemed to let the matter drop, so Ana was able to enjoy her meal and the conversation.

"So, Ana, what are your plans now that you have finished with school?" Seth asked, getting back to an earlier conversation.

"Well, I guess it all depends on what happens in Chattanooga. As I said, I don't know the extent of Father's injuries, so I'm unaware as to what kind of care he is going to require. I had thought about getting a job in town at the mercantile or something before all of this happened."

"Well, there is always a need for help here in our mercantile. Pop and I could put in a good word for you. That is, if you'd consider settling here in Shreveport."

"I do appreciate that, but I feel quite at home in Flint Creek now. I really have no desire to live anywhere else."

"Well, if you change your mind..." He let the sentence hang and gave Ana a huge smile.

"So what's the latest on Dalton? Where's he now?" Sheriff Jones wanted to know.

"He was with Father in the battle for Lookout Mountain. I haven't heard from him since." Ana felt tears sting her eyes and quickly looked down, hoping no one saw.

"That's too bad. I do hope he hasn't come to some kinda' harm." Jones shook his head. "He's a good man. I actually tried to get him to stay here to work alongside Seth and me."

"We all hope the same thing," Noah told them, reaching for Ana's hand.

When Ana was finally able to look up, she caught sight of Seth. The look in his eyes revealed his understanding of her tears. Her heart belonged to Jacob. He made no more attempts at flirting with her the rest of the meal.

They spent the rest of the afternoon getting ready for the remainder of their trip. It was time to reboard the train before Ana knew it. Seth called out as Noah was helping her up the steps of the car.

"Ana!"

Noah helped her back down onto the platform as Seth made his way to their side.

"I was wondering if I could have a quick word with you before you go?"

"Yes, of course."

It was the least Ana felt she could do. She let him lead her to the end of the platform for a little privacy.

"Ana, I want to apologize for the way I acted earlier."

"What do you mean?"

"I was flirting pretty heavy, and I shouldn't have. I mean, I didn't know you and Jacob were together."

"That's right, you didn't know. Therefore, there's no need for an apology. It's not like you did anything inappropriate."

He dropped his eyes briefly. "You're a beautiful woman, Ana—and a very special one. Jacob is one lucky man."

This made her blush. "Thank you. That's very sweet of you to say."

"I do hope he is all right and comes home to you soon."

"Me too."

He then took Ana by the hand, placed a gentle kiss to it, and began leading her back to Noah and the waiting train.

Noah spoke up over the card game he was playing after they had been riding for a while. "Seth had eyes for you, didn't he?"

"Yes, I believe he did."

"What about you? What did you think of him?"

"He seemed to be a nice man." Ana paused. "I know what you are fishing for, Noah. My heart is with Jacob. I have never been so sure of anything in my life."

"I hope you know that Jacob feels the same way about you."

"Yes, I do." She could hold back the tears no longer.

"Oh, Ana, I'm sorry. I shouldn't have said anything." He left his card game and went to her side.

"No, it's fine. I'm so worried about him, that's all."

"He's very capable. And I have every faith that he'll be all right and you will hear from him soon."

"I hope so. I can't stand this not knowing."

"Remember, God is in control. He'll bring him back to you."

Ana had never heard Noah talk this way, or any of his family for that matter. Noah noticed her surprise.

"We do believe in God, Ana. We even go to church. Just not the church in town."

"Where do you go then?"

"We have a small church gathering every Sunday on the ranch."

"I had no idea." How, after all this time, did she not know this?

Noah smiled. "You should visit sometime."

"I would like that." Ana wiped the tears from her face.

"Good, we would love to have you."

"Thanks again for coming with me. I know it has to be hard for you to be away from Beth and Isaiah."

"It is hard, but Beth and I wouldn't have any other way."

"Well, I owe you both so much!" Ana gave Noah a quick hug and sent him back to his game.

Keeping boredom at bay during the rest of the trip proved to be a full-time task. Noah taught Ana how to play the unladylike games of poker and blackjack, and Ana taught him go fish. They both felt it was a little childish, but it helped to pass the time.

Ana actually read two novels on their trip, and Noah carved several toy animals for Isaiah. Finally, after almost a whole week, they made it to Chattanooga! The fear inside Ana almost made her want to turn around and head back to Texas. What was going to happen when they stepped off the train?

22

January 1, 1864
Chattanooga

SEVERAL UNION SOLDIERS met Ana and Noah the night before when they arrived in Chattanooga. They escorted them to a waiting carriage that took them to the mayor's mansion in the center of town. The Union had commandeered the house and was now using it for their headquarters.

Once inside the house, they were led by a butler up the wide winding staircase. They made their way down a long hallway to two bedrooms situated across the hall from each other. The butler informed them the rooms were to be theirs during their visit. The gentleman also told them General Clark wanted to meet with them right after breakfast.

Neither could imagine why such a powerful officer of the Union Army would want to meet with them. The anticipation was almost unbearable.

After breakfast, the butler instructed them to wait outside two massive double doors while he went inside to announce their arrival. The solid oak doors boasted a deep dark stain, and ornate carvings covered the surfaces. For a split second, Ana lost herself in the detailed workmanship.

"Ms. Lawson," the butler began as he reentered the hallway, "the general is ready to meet with you."

"Thank you, sir." Ana and Noah followed him through the doors and into a richly decorated library.

General Clark stood behind a large wooden desk at the end of the room. He gave them a huge smile before he made his way to their side. Ana and Noah stood as still as stone and waited.

"Ah, finally," he began as he offered his hand in greeting, "I get to meet the daughter of James Lawson."

Ana shook his hand, taken aback by his informal manner. Thankfully, she was able to quickly compose herself. "It is a pleasure to meet you," she told him. "This is my chaperone, Noah. He graciously offered to accompany me on this trip."

"Noah, it's wonderful to meet you." The general shook Noah's hand. "I trust the trip here was pleasant for the both of you."

"Yes, it was," Ana and Noah agreed in unison.

"I trust your accommodations are suitable?"

"Yes, more than suitable," Ana assured him. "Thank you."

"You are most welcome, my dear. Anything for James."

"Pardon me, sir, but you act as though you know my father personally."

"Oh no, my apologies, for I should have already filled you in on our acquaintance. Your father and I were at West Point together. I still count him among my closest and dearest friends. It troubled me so when I learned of his fate at Craven House."

"It did me as well. It still does. Father has not been very forthcoming with the extent of his injuries. Perhaps you could enlighten me?"

"You don't know *anything* about them?"

"Only that he had been shot several times."

Clark dropped his head, causing Ana's heart to speed up. *What has Father been hiding?*

The general took a deep breath and looked back at her. "Your father never was very good at sharing personal matters. However, I feel it is in your best interest for you to be fully aware of what you'll find when you go to him. He will probably not appreciate me telling you, but..." He let the sentence drift off and motioned for the servant waiting just outside the doorway. "Bring us a pot of coffee, would you please? Then see to it we are not disturbed."

"Yes, sir, right away, sir."

"Come, let us take a seat." General Clark motioned for Ana and Noah to lead the way to the sitting area.

The butler served them coffee a short time after they took their seats. He then took his leave and shut the massive doors behind him.

"Ms. Lawson…," Clark began.

"Please, call me Ana."

"All right, Ana it is," he said with a smile. "The reports that you heard were true. Your father came very close to losing his life altogether. Thankfully, his wounds are healing very well." He took a deep breath. "However, your father lost one of his legs."

Ana sat in stunned silence, until she felt Noah's hand on her shoulder. "He…lost…a leg?"

"His right one. Just below the knee. Doctors have already fitted him with an artificial one. I know I don't have to tell you, but he is a very proud man. While he is doing well adjusting to the change physically, he is having somewhat of a hard time mentally. The whole ordeal has been very taxing on him in that regard."

"When can I see him?"

"As soon as you like. He's here, actually."

Ana jumped to her feet. "He's here? I must go to him at once."

The general stood as well and led her and Noah from the room. Clark explained how her father came to be at the mansion as they walked back down the long hallway.

"I simply could not bear the thought of him being alone in that hospital. Therefore, I had him brought here. He has his own private room, servants, and a private nurse."

They rounded the corner, and the general pointed to a doorway. Ana suddenly felt light-headed. Her father could be right on the other side.

"Thank you, for all you have done for my father," Ana told the general.

"You are most welcome. Please, let me know if there is anything else I can do for any of you."

Ana and Noah turned their attention back to the door in front of them and to the reason they were here.

"Are you going to be all right, Ana?" Noah had quietly waited while she learned of her father's fate but now voiced his concern.

"Yes, I think so. It's so much to take in."

"Yes, it is."

"Pray with me before I go in there."

"I would be happy to."

They joined hands and began to pray, and once finished, Ana turned to face the door.

"I will wait out here. If you need me, just call out," Noah told her.

"Thank you, Noah." Ana took a deep breath and reached for the door.

She looked anxiously around the room but found no one. There was another door at the rear of the room, and Ana considered going through it, but the fear of the unknown held her back. She stayed where she was and hoped it would not take long before someone came in.

In an attempt to calm her nerves, Ana walked around the room, taking in every detail—it didn't help. What was her father going to say when he saw her? Would he be angry with her for coming? Would he allow her to even help him?

These questions, and many more, swirled through her mind. She had no idea what was going to happen. However, she determined herself to trust in the Lord to help her through it.

"Ana?"

Ana spun around, startled by the sound of her name, and witnessed her father wheeling into the room.

"Father!" Ana rushed to his side. She threw her arms around him when she reached him and held on for dear life.

"Ana, what are you doing here?"

"I had to come, Father!" Her words came a little faster than she had planned. "I know you are probably upset with me for doing so, but I had to! Lucy and I have been so worried!"

"I am fine, Ana. Are you here alone? Josie is not the woman I thought her to be if she sent you on such a journey by yourself!"

"Oh no, Father," she began to explain, "I'm not alone. And Josie is wonderful! We have really enjoyed our time with her."

"Well, who is with you then?"

"His name is Noah. He helps run Josie's ranch. He agreed to come with me since Josie and Thomas only recently wed."

"I shall meet him later." He looked a little troubled.

"Father, are you sure you are all right? I could fetch the nurse for you."

"No, no, I am fine, really. I am overwhelmed you are here, that's all. I was not ready for you to see me this way." He then hung his head.

Ana reached for him and took his face in her hands. "Father, we will get through this. You are the strongest and bravest man I have ever known. Nothing has ever been able to keep you down."

The tiniest of smiles formed on her father's lips. "You sound exactly like your mother."

"Good! She wouldn't have let you give up, and I am not about to either!" Ana gave a smile of her own and stood and headed for the door.

"Where are you going?"

"It's time for you to meet Noah."

Ana spent the next little while filling her father in on her and Lucy's life in Texas. Her father then began to get acquainted with Noah. Thankfully, they seemed to get along splendidly. Ana noticed her father would never allow himself to stay at the center of attention for very long. He always managed to change the subject and never completely answered any question asked of him. It was obvious he was having a hard time with what had happened to him and was doing his best to pretend that it had not.

"So how long are you two in town for?" James asked his daughter.

Ana and Noah glanced at each other. "We're only in town for a week. We already have *our* tickets to take *us* back to Texas."

James caught on quickly. "*Our* tickets? Ana, I am not going to Texas with you."

"Why ever not?" she asked, trying her best to remain calm.

"My life is here. I cannot leave."

"Begging your pardon, Father, but I believe your life is in Texas. I mean, that is where Lucy and I are. What could possibly be keeping you in Chattanooga?"

"Well…I…uh …," he sputtered, knowing he had no argument. He let out a huge sigh. "Josie doesn't need a cripple underfoot."

"First of all, never call yourself that! Second, Josie is the main one insisting that you come."

"I would be in the way."

"I assure you that you would not. Josie has a spare house on the ranch, and it is ready and waiting for you to move in."

"I don't know, Ana."

"We are prepared to take you back with us, and I will *not* be taking no for an answer."

"Ana Grace! I will not have you talking to me in such a way!"

Ana dropped her head at her father's harsh tone, knowing she had crossed the line. "Father, I'm sorry. Truly, I am." Ana felt the tears begin to sting her eyes. "You are right. I shouldn't talk to you in that way. But you have always taken care of Lucy and me. And now you need us to take care of you."

"And you are merely doing the best you know how to do." James let out a sigh. "I'm sorry, Ana. I guess I'm not really sure how I am supposed to act with all of this either."

"Oh, Father!" Ana rushed to him, and they wrapped their arms around each other. "We will get through this. I know everything is going to be all right."

"Yes, yes, it is. I guess it is best I go back to Texas with you and Noah until I heal. Then we can make plans to head back to Chattanooga."

"Father, once you see the ranch, you may not want to come back to Chattanooga."

"We will see about that."

Ana couldn't believe it had actually been so easy. She had been afraid her father was going to put up a huge fight over going back with them. He did put up a little one but had given in rather quickly. Ana hoped he would find his way back to the Lord just as easily.

They all had dinner that evening with General Clark. He and Ana's father shared stories from their days together at West Point, and Noah filled them in on life on the ranch. Ana shared a few stories of her own but never really got into the conversation. Her mind was elsewhere.

Noah and her father kept looking at her from time to time, and she could tell they knew exactly what she was thinking. Neither of them felt brave enough to say anything, however. Ana made up her mind. She would ask about Jacob as soon as supper was over and she had a private moment with her father.

They all adjourned to the sitting room for coffee not long after the meal. The men talked on for a while, and then Noah and General Clark excused themselves for the night. Ana and her father sat in silence. Both seemed afraid to begin a conversation. Finally, Ana worked up the nerve and dove in headfirst.

"Father, where is Jacob?" Ana twisted the handkerchief she was holding tighter and tighter.

"Ana, I was hoping you could tell me." Concern washed over her father's face.

"You don't know what happened to him? Did he not save you from the fighting and get you to the doctors?"

"Yes, it was him and his friend Caleb Johnson. But they headed back up the mountain and back to the fighting. I thought sure he had contacted you by now."

"I haven't heard from him since the middle of November. The letter I received from him was dated for the first of November." Ana began to cry, terror washing over her. Where was he?

James rolled his chair up beside his daughter and reached to take her hand. "We will find him, Ana. I promise."

"We simply must, Father!"

"I will have William to help in the search. I know he won't mind."

"Thank you," Ana told him through her tears.

"I know how you feel about him."

"You know?"

"Yes, I know. I spoke to Jacob about the two of you the day before the battle. He cares deeply for you and assured me that you felt the same for him. I also gave him my blessing."

"Oh, Father!" Ana could not bear it any longer and allowed herself to crumble into her father's strong and comforting arms.

"My baby girl," he whispered as he stroked her hair. "All this time without any word from him has probably been dreadful for you."

"I don't know what I will do if something has happened to him!"

"There, there. I am sure he is fine."

"It's been so long!"

He held her for a while longer until her tears began to subside. He spoke as he began to help dry her tear-soaked face, "Why not head on upstairs and try to get some sleep? I know William will still be in the library working. I'll go to him and see if I can get the search started."

"Please don't keep anything you may find out from me. I have to know what happened to him."

"I promise, Ana. I'll keep you informed. Now, do try to rest, my dear."

"I'll try. Good night, Father. I love you."

"I love you too."

Ana then headed toward the stairs to her room, knowing all the while it was going to be a horribly long night.

"Can you spare a moment?" James wheeled himself into the library where his friend and a few colleagues were still working.

"Yes, of course. Please, come on in," William told him and then asked the other gentlemen to give them a moment.

"What can I do for you, James?"

James began filling him in on all the details. Thankfully, it didn't take long for William to agree to do what he could to help. The general called his men back into the room as soon as James took his leave and started making plans to find Jacob.

23

Two days passed, and the only word received was that Caleb, Jacob's friend, was also missing. James and William had worked diligently day and night to locate them. However, they had only managed to locate their parents. They all lived in a small town, a little more than an hour outside of town. Ana and Noah decided to pay them a visit.

They left after breakfast with an escort of six Union soldiers. After a bumpy long ride, they finally pulled into the yard belonging to Jacob's parents. Ana's heart raced as tears threatened to overtake her.

Noah recognized her personal turmoil and squeezed her hand. "It's going to be okay."

Noah helped her from the carriage, and she stood for a moment straightening her skirts. She wanted to make sure her appearance was presentable. At least, that was what she was telling herself she was doing. Ana knew in reality she was only stalling. Noah cleared his throat to get her attention.

"Shall we?" He motioned for the front porch. Ana gave a nod and finally began to move her feet.

The front door opened just as they were reaching the bottom step. A lady, appearing to be in her late forties, stepped out, looking completely terrified. She looked at Ana and Noah and then at the soldiers who had dismounted their horses and were waiting beside the carriage. Ana realized she had to be Jacob's mother, for the resemblance was uncanny.

"Mrs. Dalton?" Ana asked.

"Yes, and who are you?" she asked warily.

"My name is Ana Grace Lawson, and this is Noah. We are hoping—"

"Ana? Ana Grace, did you say?"

"Yes, ma'am."

With that, she came off the porch and wrapped Ana up in a hug. "Oh, Ana! Jacob wrote about you in his letters. I'm so glad I'm finally getting to meet you." Mrs. Dalton pulled away and looked hopefully into Ana's eyes. "Please, tell me you have news from my son. We haven't heard from him in almost two months now."

"You haven't? Oh, I was so hoping you could tell *me* something about him. I've had no word from him either."

Mrs. Dalton's excitement quickly faded. She then turned and began walking back down the path toward the house.

"Please, come inside." She led them onto the porch and into the front room of the house.

The house, while small, was very lovely. Everything was neat as a pin. Mrs. Dalton went to the kitchen to get them some tea, and Ana looked around the room and tried to imagine Jacob in it. He told her he lived in the same place all his life, but it was hard to see him among the frill that decorated the room.

Ana noticed a couple of pictures sitting on the mantle and walked over for a closer look. One was of Jacob's mother and father on their wedding day, the other of Jacob. He was in his Confederate uniform and looked like the perfect soldier. While it was a handsome picture, it didn't seem right either. Nothing here reminded Ana of the Jacob she knew.

"Are you all right?" Noah asked as he walked up beside her.

"I'm so worried, Noah. Where is he?"

"We'll find him. I know we will."

"I so hope you're right!"

Mrs. Dalton came through the door at that moment, carrying a tray loaded with a porcelain tea service and lemon tea cakes.

"Please, have a seat, and I will pour you some tea. Then I would like to hear what you know about my son."

They spent the next couple of hours discussing the facts they had where Jacob was concerned. Ana and Noah assured her they had the support of General Clark and his officers and would eventually learn the fate of Jacob and Caleb.

Mrs. Dalton told them that Jacob's father had gone off on his own in search of information. All agreed to share any new leads they were able to come up with.

They also discussed the fact that Caleb's family needed an update whenever possible, and Mrs. Dalton volunteered for the task. They then said their good-byes, expressing their hope of getting to meet again under better circumstances. Ana and Noah then began their ride back into town.

"Oh, Noah. I so hoped she could tell us something." Ana felt defeated.

"You must not get discouraged. You must keep up hope."

"You're right. It's just so hard sometimes."

"I know it is."

They rode in silence the rest of the way back to Chattanooga.

"James! We found them!" Clark rushed into the dining room. Ana, James, and Noah had barely sat down to dinner but now waited breathlessly for the information William had come to share.

He made his way to James's side and handed him the papers he was carrying. William looked to Ana and Noah and began to explain as James opened them up and began to read.

"As you know, we had checked all the casualty lists for both the Union and Confederacy and found nothing. I even sent men up to Craven House to have a look for any sign of them and still nothing. Nothing came from any of the searches done in the hospitals around either. Today I sent several groups of men to check at the prison camps. That's where we found them! They are both alive and well and here in Chattanooga!"

This news caused Ana's heart to leap in her chest! She had never felt so much relief in all her life! Ana did the first thing that came to her mind. She raised her hands toward heaven and praised the Lord, right there in front of everyone.

"Thank you, sweet Heavenly Father! Thank you!" Ana composed herself and looked at Noah, who appeared as elated she was. She then looked at her father.

The look on his face let her know that, in his eyes, she had done something horribly wrong. The funny thing was, Ana really didn't care at that moment. She would deal with her father's beliefs—or, rather, disbeliefs—at another time. Right now, all that mattered was Jacob was alive!

"I have already taken steps toward getting them released and brought here. They should be here when you awake in the morning."

"Thank you, William, for all you have done." James shook the man's hand.

"Yes, thank you, from the bottom of my heart!" Ana could hardly contain her emotions.

Clark took his leave, and they managed to finish their meal with pleasant conversation. One could feel the underlying tension in the room, however. Ana knew it was only a matter of time before she would have to have a conversation with her father about her faith. She prayed it would go well.

Ana spent a lot of time watching out the window instead of sleeping that night. She hoped to catch a glimpse of Jacob and Caleb as they made their way to the mansion. She became more anxious as time passed and decided to say a prayer. Afterward, she took out her Bible and began to study.

She heard a commotion out on the front lawn well into the night.

"Jacob!" She rushed to the window, thinking surely they had finally arrived. However, she saw only a group of soldiers hitching their horses and heading for the door.

Ana made her way down the back staircase, closest to the library, in hopes the men were heading there. She found them all waiting around William's desk and crept as close as she could to hear what they were saying.

From her hiding place, she saw William wheeling her father down the hallway and straight into the library. She was now positive this had something to do with Jacob.

"What happened?" the general asked the men point-blank.

"Well, sir, turns out there was a Union officer at the camp who went renegade. He was very upset with the news the Union was going to release two of the prisoners. He enlisted the help of a small group, and they took Mr. Dalton and Mr. Johnson out of the camp under the guise of a simple transfer. Word leaked out after their departure. Their intent is to take the *gray scum*—as they called them—far away from the area and give them exactly what they deserve. Again, their words, not mine, sir."

When the soldier finished talking, Ana realized her whole body shook.

"Where were they headed?" James asked.

"Southwest is all we are sure of. They managed to leave out shortly after our men left this morning. Therefore, they have several hours' head start on us."

"Get supplies together, and the six of you head out. Let me know if you hear anything else. Let me know when you start to leave. We have to find those men! And when you do"—Clark's voice began to grow angry—"I want those *so-called* soldiers of ours arrested and brought straight to me!"

"Yes, sir."

The group of soldiers made their exit, and Ana quietly retreated up to her room, where she spent the next several hours on her knees.

"Ana? Ana, wake up," Noah said as he pounded on the door.

Ana slowly opened her eyes to a dimly lit room and then sat straight up with a jolt. She jumped out of bed, threw on her robe, and headed for the door, all the while praying Noah had brought good news.

"Noah, did they find Jacob?" Ana asked as soon as she jerked open the door.

"No, not yet." He paused. "Wait. How did you know?"

"I overheard the soldiers telling Father and William last night."

Noah nodded in understanding. "As I said, they haven't found them, but they do know where they are headed."

"Where?"

"You are not going to believe this. They are headed to a little town east of Shreveport, a place called Hinkley."

"Surely, you must be joking!" Ana could hardly fathom what she was hearing.

"Turns out the leader of the group who took them has family there. They are big slave sympathizers and have caused all kinds of problems. They operate a branch of the Underground Railroad and have even gone so far as to sneak onto plantations to help the slaves escape.

"The authorities have been trying to catch them at this for years. It seems they are always one step ahead of the law. I really don't want to tell you this part, but some of the family is also accused of killing a slave owner a couple of years ago."

"Oh my! And now they have Jacob and Caleb!" Ana suddenly became very light-headed. She quickly sought the edge of her bed, and Noah rushed to her side.

"Are you all right?" He placed his hands on her shoulders to steady her.

"Yes, I think so. I can't believe this is happening. What are Father and the general doing about all of this?"

"They have sent men after them. And I sent out a telegram to Sheriff Jones and Seth to see if there was anything they could do to help. I hope you don't mind that I did it without asking you first."

"Oh no, Noah. That was a wonderful idea! I am so glad you thought to do it!"

"I only hope they can help."

"I am sure if there is anything at all they can do, they will do it. Maybe we will get word back from them soon."

"Yes, maybe." Noah then announced he would head back downstairs to allow her to get ready for the day.

"Thank you for everything," Ana told him as he made his way through the door.

"You're welcome, Ana."

Ana did not rush in getting ready that morning. She spent as much time as she possibly could in prayer, asking God to protect Caleb and her sweet Jacob.

24

January 4, 1864

THEY RECEIVED WORD from Seth later in the morning that he and his father were looking into things there. He assured them they would do whatever they had to, to get Jacob and Caleb back safe and sound.

Ana was not the patient sort, so by lunchtime, she was begging her father for them to go to Shreveport and wait there. It actually helped that Noah was also anxious. However, Ana's father convinced them to wait until they heard from Seth again. After all, they were only *somewhat* sure the gang was heading there with Jacob and Caleb. In the meantime, James sent telegrams out to all the stops between Chattanooga and Shreveport, asking the local authorities to be on the lookout.

Ana took advantage of the free time she had and visited a few of her friends still in Chattanooga. It was good to catch up with them. She also had Noah take her to see her old house—or, rather, what was left of it.

It broke Ana's heart to see the state it was in. Luckily, her father was able to salvage most of their things and had them stored somewhere in town. Ana didn't know what she would have done if he hadn't been able to do that. Everything in that house reminded her of her mother and Liza. It would have killed her if she had lost all of it.

Ana was exhausted by the end of the day. The emotional strain of the day weighed heavy on her. She excused herself as soon as it was fitting and headed off to bed. She prayed before she lay down that morning would bring good news.

Ana heard Liza's familiar words of comfort before drifting off to sleep: *Everythin's gonna be all right, you see.* Ana concentrated on these words and prayed they would prove true.

"Caleb, wake up."

"What happened?" Caleb wanted to know as he tried to sit up.

"You took the butt of a rifle to the side of your head. You've been out cold for about five hours now."

"Last thing I remember was walking onto the train. What did they hit me for anyway?"

"Who knows, with this bunch?"

"You all right?"

"Yeah, I'm fine. I wish I could figure a way out of these chains, though."

"Yeah, that *would* be nice." Caleb rubbed his pain-filled wrists.

Their captors had their wrists and ankles chained and had kept them blindfolded until they forced them into the bunk car.

They still had yet to figure out why the soldiers took them. Their captors told them it was only a transfer to another camp. Jacob began to think otherwise once they boarded the train.

Their time in the prison camp had been hard, but at least they were treated decently while there. Today, however, everything seemed different—more tense. Jacob spent his time in prayer and deep concentration while Caleb had been out cold. He had to figure out exactly what was going on. He was beginning to fear the worst and needed to work out a plan to deal with it all.

Jacob and Caleb were alone in the cramped bunk car. The soldiers guarding them had gone into the adjoining car in search of food. Jacob took this opportunity to share with Caleb his worries.

"I'm kind of thinking you're right, now that I know they whacked me in the head for no good reason. Something is definitely not right about all of this." Caleb tried to reposition himself on the tiny bunk. "Have you overheard anything that might give us some clues?"

"I'm not sure. I have overheard some of their private conversations, but nothing really has made any sense."

"What are some things you heard?"

"Well," Jacob said thoughtfully, "they said something about Louisiana. So I thought maybe that's where we're headed. But I can't tell which direction we're going since there are no windows in here."

"All right, what else?"

"They mentioned a few names. None of them rang familiar."

Caleb waited for Jacob to continue.

"Something was said about being close to the 'riverbed' or 'river red.' I was half asleep then, so I am not sure what that meant."

"What about Red River?"

"Yeah, that could be it! It's in Louisiana too!"

"It runs through Shreveport, does it not?"

"Yes, it does, and so does the railroad. I wonder—" Jacob stopped short as the soldiers made their way back into the bunk car carrying a tray of food. Their discussion would have to wait.

The two men ate in silence. They each tried their best to sort the same questions out in their minds. Where were they going? And what was going to happen to them once they got there?

"We received word from the sheriff in Meridian, Mississippi, sir." The officer said as he made his way into the dining room. It was afternoon, and they were all finishing up their meal.

"Let us have it then," the general instructed.

"The sheriff states a train came through town during the night. On board were approximately six Union soldiers, and they had two prisoners with them."

"Why did they not stop them?" the general's voice boomed with anger. "They were sent the same telegram everyone else was—to be on the lookout for these men and to stop them if they were found!"

"It seems the telegram got mixed in with some other papers and wasn't found in time, sir. The sheriff did say the train was headed on toward Shreveport."

"Get word to the sheriff there then! Tell them to be waiting when that train pulls into town! Make sure the message is delivered this time!"

"Sir, yes, sir." The young officer turned on his heels and hurried from the room.

"Incompetent idiots!" William growled.

"At least we know we were on the right track, William. We will get them when they reach Shreveport, I am sure of it," James sounded calm, but Ana knew her father. She knew he fumed with anger as well.

Ana was thankful they had Seth and Sheriff Jones to depend on. She knew they would get the job done. Ana looked to Noah and prayed silently that this would all be over soon.

Shreveport, Louisiana

"Pop, we received another telegram from Chattanooga." Seth made his way back inside the sheriff's office.

"What's it say?"

"It says they managed to get past Meridian, Mississippi, and that they are headed here. They asked we be waiting for them."

"You bet we'll be waitin'! When did they pull out of Meridian?"

"About four this morning. I checked with the depot, and they said the train was on schedule and should be getting in about ten o'clock tonight."

"Good, that gives us plenty of time to get some men rounded up. I am afraid we are going to need all the help we can get on this one. We ain't dealin' with a bunch of ruffians like before. This time, they're trained military men. They'll know exactly what they're doin'."

"I'd already thought of that. I ran into Sam and Jake on my way back here, and they agreed to help. Said it was the least they could do for what Dalton did to help everyone out around here."

"Good. Let's get outta here and see who else we round up."

With that, they both headed out into the afternoon light in search of reinforcements.

25

"ANA?" HER FATHER'S voice broke into her prayers.

Ana had excused herself shortly after lunch and spent the afternoon wandering the property and praying for Jacob and Caleb's safe return. The temperature was soon too cold for her outside in the gardens, sending her back inside the mansion. She searched and found a spot in the sunroom on the back of the house so she could continue her time of solitude. She was lost in her thoughts and jumped when she heard her name.

"Oh, Father! You scared me! I didn't hear you come in."

"I don't know how you could keep from it with all the noise this chair makes."

Ana smiled at her father's uncharacteristic attempt at sarcasm. "I was lost in thought, that's all."

"I could tell. I rather hated to interrupt you, but I wanted to make sure you were all right. I haven't seen you since lunch."

"I needed to be alone for a while."

"I know you are worried about Jacob."

"Yes, and Caleb. Have you heard anything else?"

"No, honey, I am afraid we have not. I'm sure you will hear first thing tomorrow that they are perfectly fine."

"I sure hope so. Promise me if you hear anything during the night, you will get word to me. I'm sure I won't get a wink of sleep anyway."

"I promise. Are you about ready for dinner? Cook said it would be ready in about ten minutes."

"I don't think I can eat anything. My stomach is in knots."

"Well, all right then. I will tell Cook to save you something for later—just in case."

Ana gave him a weak smile, and he turned his chair around and began heading for the door.

"Try not to worry so much, Ana Grace."

"I know the Lord is going to take care of them. I only hope I don't go daft in the process." Ana realized what she said the instant she heard her Father's chair come to a halt.

James spun his chair around to face her, and Ana braced for the attack. "What did you say?"

Ana knew she had to be honest with him. "I said the Lord was going to take care of them."

"You know how I feel about even the mention of such things, Ana!"

"I'm sorry, Father. I don't want to hurt you. However, I have to stand up for what I believe. I believe God sent His Son, Jesus, to live and then die on the cross for my sins. I have chosen to allow Him into my heart and to follow Him and His teachings."

James sat looking at his daughter for the longest time. Ana could tell he was trying to figure out how best to handle her confession of faith. Suddenly, out of nowhere, his countenance softened.

"I don't know what to say, Ana. You know how I feel, how I have felt since your mother passed. Nevertheless, for the life of me, I cannot summon up the energy to be angry with you. I still don't agree with your decision. However, I know your mother would be pleased, and that matters a great deal to me. What about Lucy? Does she feel the same way as you?"

"She does feel the same way, Father. However, she has yet to experience salvation. But I know it is only a matter of time."

James hung his head in defeat. Ana's heart ached for him. She really didn't want to hurt him, but he had to know the truth.

He sat there for a moment and then turned his chair around and quietly left the room. Ana sat stunned by what had happened. She was glad it was out in the open now. To see the hurt on her father's face was almost too much to bear, however.

Noah appeared in the doorway. "Are you all right?" Worry showed on his face.

"You heard?"

"Yes, I heard." He walked over and took a seat beside her on the chaise.

"I hurt him, Noah." She began to cry.

"Ana, are you sorry for what you believe?"

"No, of course not! Nothing could ever make me sorry for believing and loving my Lord. For He saved from an eternity in torment!"

"Good. Keep trusting in Him, and He will help bring your father around."

"I know you're right. At least I can say that went a lot better than I had expected it to. I expected him to really be furious." Ana dropped her head. "Actually, I think that would have been easier. I mean, I was prepared for that."

Jacob and Caleb almost fell out of the bunks they were lying in as the train came to a screeching halt. They scrambled as best as they could to right themselves. However, thanks to the chains that bound their hands and feet, it proved to be a hard task.

"You all right, Jacob?" Caleb asked as he steadied himself against the wall.

"Yeah, I am fine. You?"

"Yeah. What are we stopping like that for, I wonder?"

The door of the adjoining car banged open, and the sound of heavy footsteps on the connector began echoing through the bunk car.

"It looks like we may be about to find out," Jacob offered.

The bunk-car door flung open, and four of the Union soldiers rushed inside. They then began to drag Jacob and Caleb out into the cold, wet night.

"Where are we?" Caleb got another whack on the head for asking. At least they didn't knock him out cold this time.

Jacob kept quiet and prayed for his friend. He also scanned the countryside, trying to make out something familiar. Unfortunately, the night was so pitch-black there was nothing to be seen anywhere. They were out in the middle of nowhere—no depot, nothing!

The men led them to an awaiting covered wagon and forced them into the back of it. Inside was a man and a young boy, who couldn't have been more than ten years old, both brandishing shotguns. It was obvious they were not soldiers. This caused the questions in both Jacob's and Caleb's minds to multiply by a thousand. This whole thing was getting more bizarre by the second.

The wagon began to move with a jerk, and they could hear the train starting back up as well. They looked at each other. They had to figure a way out of this and fast. It was becoming painfully clear their lives depended on it.

Jacob worked up the nerve to speak after they had been riding for a while. "Where are we?"

"Hinkley," the youngest of their hosts began. The older one slapped him in the back of the head with his hand.

"Keep your stupid mouth shut, Levi! They don't need to know nothin'! I swear I told Jonas he was makin' a mistake lettin' a little snot-nosed brat like you come along tonight!"

He finished his attack on the young boy and then turned his attention to Jacob. "And you—you need to just sit over there and keep *your* mouth shut too!"

Jacob and Caleb exchanged glances and then continued to work silently on a plan for escape.

"Sorry, Jed." Levi hung his head in embarrassment.

So we're in Hinkley, Louisiana, Jacob thought. *What do I know about Hinkley?* Jacob let his mind wander on that thought for a few minutes. *Nothing. Absolutely nothing! Nothing, except it's in Louisiana and close to Shreveport and Red River, which was no help at all!*

Jacob grew more frustrated and decided he needed to spend some time in prayer. He couldn't allow himself to get angry. He had to keep a clear head, and he trusted in the Lord to help him with that.

26

Shreveport, 9:30 p.m.

"THE LAST OF them men just arrived, Pop," Seth told his father.

"Good!" the sheriff exclaimed. "How many does that make again?"

"Counting us, there are twenty."

Jones nodded, pleased with the number. "I think it's a good idea for us to head on over to the depot and get ready. The train could actually be on time."

Both men shared a chuckle over his sarcasm and then headed out the door.

The sheriff gave out orders once everyone had gathered at the depot. He sent men off in different directions in hopes of covering every possible angle once the train came to a stop. He, Seth, and a few of the others took up guard on the platform. They planned to be the first ones on the train. The rest of the men were to storm the other exits. For now, they waited.

James kept to himself for the rest of the afternoon. Ana knew he was very upset with her for her expression of faith. Nevertheless, she believed in her heart they would be able to work everything out eventually. She had prayed all afternoon for that very thing. It would just take time, and she was willing to give him that.

It was now almost nine-thirty, and Ana knew the train was supposed to be pulling into Shreveport soon. She also knew someone waited at the telegraph office in town to bring word on Jacob and Caleb as soon as it came in. Ana decided to find her father and wait alongside him. She wanted to receive the information as soon as he did.

Ana found William, Noah, and her father in deep conversation when she entered the library. They each looked up when they heard her. She could tell by their strained expressions that they still hadn't heard anything. Ana walked over and sat on the window seat and began watching the sporadic fall of snow.

"You all right, Ana?" Noah wanted to know.

"Yes, as well as I can be, anyway."

They sat in silence, each lost in their own thoughts. The grandfather clock struck ten o'clock and caused them both to jump. Noah stood and began to pace the library nervously. Ana refused to take her eyes off the front lawn, for she hoped to see exactly when the soldiers arrived with news from the depot.

"It's past ten! Where's that fool train!" Seth paced back and forth across the platform.

"Calm down, Seth," his father tried. "You know how it is with trains. They ain't never on time."

"Yeah, well…this one needs to get a move on!" Seth continued his march.

Another fifteen minutes passed. Finally they began to hear the faint sounds of the approaching train.

Sheriff Jones yelled out to his men, "Get ready now, boys! This thing's gonna go down fast!"

The train rounded the bend at that moment and began to slow. The men began to rush on board before it had even come to a complete stop. Seth, with guns drawn, was first to enter the passenger car. The sheriff and two other men followed him. The car was empty.

Seth motioned toward the adjoining bunk car, and they quickly made their way in that direction. They made their way out and on to the connector. The sheriff moved to the front of the line, jerked open the sliding door, and allowed Seth and the others to storm the car. Some of their own men entered through the back door at the same time, and the two groups met in the middle.

They began searching behind the curtains of each bunk, finding them all empty.

"Where are they?" Seth shouted in frustration.

"You men head back out and double-check up and down and make sure no one's hidin' in those livestock cars back there. I'm going to have a little talk with the engineer and coal man," the sheriff ordered.

The men hurriedly made their way back outside. Everyone except Seth, that is. Something was telling him to search the bunks again. He went over the two lower bunks and took in every little detail. Then, on a whim, he tore the bedding out of one. There, carved into the wood, he found these words:

SIX MEN. ARMED. CLUES LEAD TO RED RIVER. NOT MUCH ELSE. JD

They were here!

Seth tore out of the train and rushed straight into the depot where his father was interrogating the engineer.

"We know you had to stop somewhere and let them off!" Jones yelled at the man. "Where was it?"

"I ain't tellin' you nothin'!" The engineer snarled back at him.

The raging deputy jerked the man to his feet and slammed him into the side of the counter. "Well, you might not tell him anything," Seth began his berating, "but you will dang well tell me!"

Seth emphasized his point with a strong punch to the man's gut. The engineer let out a loud groan and a rush of air. He then fell to his knees, only to have Seth hoist him in the air and slam him to the floor in the corner of the room.

"Now get to talkin'!" Seth growled.

Seth knew by the fear in the engineer's eyes that he definitely had the upper hand. He was confident he would eventually get the information he wanted. Sometimes his size and strength really came in handy.

Even though the snow was falling heavier now, it was still too warm for any of it to stick to the ground. Ana allowed the sight of it falling and the peaceful ticktock of the clock to calm her nerves. It was now almost eleven-thirty, and they still had no word from the depot.

Noah still quietly paced the floor. William worked attentively on something at the desk, and James had rolled himself over to the reading area in an attempt to occupy his mind with Shakespeare.

Suddenly Ana caught a glimpse of movement at the end of the drive. "Someone is coming!" she announced as the rider made his way up to the front of the house.

They all scrambled and waited patiently while the soldier made his way into the room.

"Sir," he began, addressing William, "the mission has failed. The authorities in Shreveport stormed the train as soon as it pulled into the depot only to find it empty."

"No, this isn't happening!" Ana felt her knees begin to buckle.

Noah rushed to her side and put his arm around her waist in an attempt to keep her upright.

"I assume the engineer and coal man have been questioned," William fumed.

"Yes, sir," the soldier assured him. "They managed to get a location out of the engineer as to where he stopped the train for them to disembark. He said it was near Hinkley. He also verified there were six Union soldiers and two prisoners. The deputy has taken a large group of men to investigate. That is all the news I have at this time."

"Very well then," William told him. "Head back to the depot. I want to know as soon as you hear anything else."

The soldier saluted and turned to leave. James called out to him before he reached the library door. "Let the sheriff in Shreveport know that I am getting a train ready and will be headed there as soon as possible."

"Yes, sir." With that, the soldier was out the door.

James looked at Ana and Noah and spoke, "You two need to get your things ready."

"James, I want you to take a few of my men with you," William told his friend.

"That isn't necessary, William."

"I insist."

"Very well. Thank you for all you have done in this matter, but most of all, for what you have done for me personally."

"James, it has been my pleasure. If you need anything else, you let me know."

James motioned for Ana and Noah to follow him from the room. They then headed off to ready their things for the trip.

Jacob and Caleb spent their time in the back of the wagon trying to peer through the small rips in the cover. They hoped to get a glimpse of anything that would let them know where they were headed. They had ended up on a road running alongside the river. And from the stars Jacob could see, he knew they were going north. But north to where?

Jacob looked at the two men in the wagon with them. The older of the two seemed very serious and intent on the mission at hand while the younger seemed more anxious. And by the looks of pity and fear he kept sending Jacob and Caleb's way, he seemed to have a small spark of compassion where the other one had none. Jacob decided this young man might be worth befriending. That little bit of compassion might come in handy.

After what seemed like an eternity in that wagon, it suddenly slowed to a stop. Jed motioned for Levi to go first out of the wagon. He then began waving his shotgun at Caleb. "Now you," he ordered Caleb to move.

Caleb followed the order, and then it was Jacob's turn. They began scanning the area as soon as they were out of the wagon.

They were in the backyard of a huge plantation-style home flanked by several smaller buildings. One of which was a massive two-story barn. Their captors led them inside the barn and toward the back to the tack room. A couple of men moved a worktable out away from the wall, revealing a secret door in the floor of the barn. The door opened to a cool dark pit.

They released Jacob and Caleb from their chains and then forced them at gunpoint into the pit. They went willing down the rickety ladder only to have it snatched up as soon as they reached the damp bottom.

The lumber lining the inside of the pit helped a little in keeping them warm. Only a little bit, however. At least they didn't have to contend with the cold breezes from outside.

The men tossed in a couple of blankets and a cloth sack containing food. They then lowered down a bucket of water and closed the door down on top of them. They could hear the clink of a padlock and then the worktable moving back into position. Both waited until they were sure they were alone to speak.

"Well, this is *so* much better!" Caleb sarcastically referred to their new accommodations.

"At least we are not being bounced all over the place," Jacob pointed out. "And we are out of those infernal chains!"

"Yeah, you're right." Caleb rubbed his red swollen wrists. "I'm starved. Let's see what is in the bag."

"Then we need to start trying to figure a way out of this place." Jacob helped his friend search the sack.

"You find anything out that way?" Seth asked.

"Nope, not a thing."

He had carried several men with him out along the tracks where the engineer said he had stopped the train. He was hoping to get a good lead as to where the Union soldiers headed with Jacob and his friend. So far, they had found nothing. He was beginning to believe the engineer hadn't been truthful with the location.

"I haven't found anything either. Not so much as a hoofprint. I think we need to head back into town and have another heart-to-heart with our little friend the engineer."

27

January 6, 1864

THE TRAIN ROLLED into town about ten o'clock in the morning. It had been the longest thirty-four hours of Ana's life. She was so glad her father had secured a private car for her. She really needed the time alone. And there was no need for everyone to endure her troubled mood.

She was so worried about Jacob and Caleb. She could think of nothing else. Ana prayed the whole way that Seth and Sheriff Jones had good news for them when they arrived. The time had finally come for them to find out.

Ana felt she could not get off the train fast enough. She stood and quickly made her way to the main car as soon as the train came to a complete stop. Her father, Noah, and a host of Union soldiers met her there.

The men assisted James off the train and, after steadying him on his crutches, cleared the path, allowing Ana to disembark. Noah followed, and they then made their way into the depot. The sight of the soldiers caused everyone to stop and stare.

James addressed the baggage clerk who had rushed to greet them. "Please see that all of our things are taken over to the hotel. They should be expecting us."

"Yes, sir." The young man set out to do as instructed.

"Father, are you all right?" Ana was worried about him overdoing it and could tell by his weary expression that he was getting tired.

"Yes, Ana, I am fine," he assured her. "Let me catch my breath, and then we will go to the sheriff's office."

"Please try not to do too much. We don't need you getting ill."

"I will go on to the hotel for some rest after I speak with the sheriff."

"That sounds like a wonderful idea."

James traded his crutches for his wheelchair and indulged in a quick reprieve. They soon were on their way out of the depot and into the bright January sun.

Luckily, the boardwalk would carry them all the way through town. They would only have to cross the street once. This proved to be a large task with James's chair. Thankfully, there were plenty of strong men there to help.

Seth stepped out of the sheriff's office and spotted them as soon as they made it to the other side. He rushed down the boardwalk as quickly as his long legs would carry him.

"We weren't expecting you until tonight," he told Ana. "We would have been at the depot to meet you had we known."

"No worries. We were able to get started earlier than we had expected."

"It's good to see you." He gave her a tender smile. His look quickly turned serious, however. "I only wish it was under better circumstances."

"Yes, as do I. Seth, you remember Noah."

"Noah, how are you?" Seth extended his hand toward the man.

"I'm fine, and you?" Noah answered as he shook the man's hand.

"Good," he answered simply before returning his attention to Ana.

"Seth, I would like for you to meet my father, Major General James Lawson. Father, this is Deputy Sheriff Seth Jones."

The two men shook hands.

"It's a pleasure to meet you, sir," Seth told James.

"The pleasure is all mine, Deputy."

"Why don't we get you all inside now before you freeze?" Seth suggested.

They followed him the rest of the way down the boardwalk and into the sheriff's office. Sheriff Jones was working behind the desk and stood as they entered. After introductions, they spent the next hour listening to all the details Seth and his men were able to uncover.

Seth told them how the engineer had given false information as to where he had stopped the train. Unfortunately, that was all he was able to get out of him. The engineer refused to say anything more. However, with a little "persuasion," the coal man had finally talked and had given the correct spot of the drop-off.

Seth had carried several men out there the day before. They found wagon tracks and several sets of horse tracks all heading north. They had followed those tracks for about five miles. It was getting late in the day by then, so they decided to head back to town. They had readied supplies to go back out as soon as Ana and the others arrived with the extra men.

"I believe we have everything we need for the trip all ready to go. We'll set out as soon as you are ready," Seth addressed the soldiers.

"We are ready to go whenever you are, Deputy," Capitan Cartwright assured him.

Cartwright was to be in charge of the others while they were on this mission.

"Very well then. You all go on over to the hotel and get your things settled. I will round up my men and meet you there."

"Yes, sir."

With that, everyone made ready to leave.

"Seth?"

"Yes, Noah?"

"Do you have a spare horse I could borrow? I want to come with you."

"Got one already saddled up for you. I kinda expected you'd want to."

Jacob and Caleb had been working diligently over the last several hours. They had discovered that a few of the planks on the wall of the pit were loose enough to take down. They had decided the location of the pit was along the outside wall of the barn, so their plan—a tunnel.

They were going to dig and come out into the thick stand of brush, which they had both seen growing all the way up to the side of the barn.

Levi had been the only person who had even been back out there to check on them. He had made sure they had plenty to eat and had even brought a couple more blankets. Thankfully, once their digging had begun, Levi had only barely opened the door far enough to toss in the items, so he never saw what was going on inside. It was obvious he was afraid of what the others would do to him if they caught him. He would whisper a quick, "Here you go, boys," and never stuck around long enough to be thanked for his efforts.

"Man, I wish we had something besides this cup to dig with!" Caleb complained. "We could have been out of here already!"

"Yeah, I know. You want me to take over for a while?"

"I can go a while longer." Caleb went headfirst back into the tunnel they were creating.

They had managed to dig the tunnel in about five feet and had it about four feet in diameter. They decided to go at a slight angle and estimated to come out around five feet into the woods. However, with only a drinking cup and a cloth sack to work with, it was going to be a slow go. At least Levi had supplied them with a lantern and oil. They could at least see what they were doing.

Later that day, they heard some men come into the barn. They listened as closely as they could to their hushed conversation in hopes of figuring out some of the mess they were in.

"So when is Silas planning on doing it?" one of the men asked.

"Day after tomorrow," the other answered. "The boss is supposed to get into town tomorrow night, and they want to get it taken care of as soon as possible after that."

"Have they got everything ready?"

"Yeah, they were putting the finishing touches on the grandstand earlier."

"They sure are making a big deal out of this, ain't they?"

"Of course, they are! I mean, how often is it that we get to hang a couple Confederate scums?"

"So true!" The two men chuckled and then made their way out of the barn.

Jacob and Caleb stood in shock at what they had just heard. Neither of them wanted to face the fact that *they* were the *Confederate scum*. A new sense of urgency swept through them both.

Caleb began to pace back and forth in their small prison as Jacob scrambled back inside the tunnel to continue the dig.

"We gotta get outta here, Jacob!"

"I know, Caleb! Believe me, I know! We still have at least another day and a half worth of digging to do too."

"Yep, looks like it's going to be a long night."

"You're right about that. Caleb, you have to keep up hope. God is going to see us through this."

"I know He will. Now quit talking so much and get back to digging," Caleb teased, trying to lighten the mood.

Jacob chuckled and tossed a handful of dirt back in his friend's direction.

"Missed me!"

"Whose place is that?" Noah wanted to know.

They had been riding all day and had finally made it to what appeared to be a run-down plantation. They were spying on the place from a small ridge to the south of the main house.

"That's Carl Phillips's place," Seth informed him. "That's right, ain't it, Hank?"

"Yep, that's right." Hank, one of the sheriff's oldest and dearest friends, had agreed to come with them to help them find the plantation. "Meanest ol' devil I ever knowed."

"Mean?" Noah asked, wanting clarification.

Hank continued, "He's a transplanted Northerner and real big in the Underground Railroad. He used to give the other plantation owners aroun' here a lot of trouble. He would send his men out, and they would sneak into neighborin' slave-ownin' plantations. They'd kidnap slaves and bring 'em here and help 'em go on and escape." He bit off a huge plug of his tobacco.

"They also been accused of burnin' down a few barns here and there." He spat out a mouthful of spit and continued, "I guess the worst thing was about two years ago when the Latham's home burned to the groun'."

"Yeah," Seth agreed and then took over the telling of the story. "That was bad. They found Latham hanging from a tree in the backyard and his wife and youngest child's bodies in the rubble of the house. Thankfully, their other three children were at school. Everyone knew who did it too. There's never been any real evidence to back it up, though, so it remains an unsolved case."

"I tell ya, he is lower 'an a snake in a wagon rut!" Hank added, "Makes me sick to know they ain't havin' ta pay for what they did!"

"Well, they ain't paying yet, lawfully speaking, but they have suffered financially," Seth pointed out. "So many people believe they killed Latham and his family that they quit doing business with them. Their farming business has completely failed. The land the house and barn sit on is all that's left. They've had to sell off everything else. About a thousand acres from what I've heard."

"So do you think they could have done this? Do you think they have Jacob and Caleb?" Noah wanted to know.

"Sounds like somethin' they'd do, that's for sure," Hank said with another spit to the ground. "Well, since I helped ya find the place, I'm gonna head on back. I'm too old to get caught up in any gunplay."

"Thanks, Hank." Seth patted him on the back.

"Any time." The old man then turned his horse and headed for home.

Seth turned back to Noah. "We will hang out here until it gets dark, and then we'll go in and investigate. If they're there, we'll find 'em," Seth assured him.

28

"Ugh, this waiting is killing me!" Ana sat down on one of the empire sofas in the common room of the hotel.

Seth and Noah had been out on their search since before lunch. It was now well past dinnertime. In fact, had she been at home and her life a little more settled, Ana would be thinking about heading to bed soon. As it was, she was not sure she would ever sleep again.

"Patience, my dear, patience," James said in an attempt to comfort his daughter.

She had been trying to be patient all day. All attempts had failed, however, so she decided to do the only thing she had been able to do—pray.

Ana closed her eyes and began to talk to the Lord. She opened her eyes slowly when her prayer was over and did feel somewhat better. That was until she realized her father was watching her.

The look in his eyes made Ana's heart wrench. She couldn't be sure if it was anger, confusion, hurt, concern, or a twisted mix of all of the above. She suddenly felt brave enough to ask, "Is there something wrong, Father?"

"What were you doing just now?"

"Praying Seth and Noah would be able to find Jacob and Caleb and that all of this would soon be over. Also, that everyone would be safe and well."

James hung his head. "Where exactly has all of this come from, Ana? You know how I feel about it."

"Yes, Father, I do know how you feel. But I also know how I feel."

To this, he simply shook his head. After a few moments, he continued, "When did this start?"

"My believing?"

"Yes."

"I guess I have always believed. We used to be in church every chance we got, and I learned a lot during those times. Since Mama died…," Ana hesitated slightly, judging his reaction to the subject of her mother's death, "I haven't thought much about it. It all started coming back to me when we were getting ready to leave Chattanooga. The day it went under attack."

Ana felt the need to tell him the whole story. Therefore, she did. She told him about praying with Liza and about Jacob witnessing to her. She shared about going to church with Josie. Finally, the best part of all, her salvation.

James sat quietly and listened to everything Ana had to say, weighing every word. Finally, after a few minutes, she was surprised to see the hint of a tear in his eye. He never said a word, only sat looking at his daughter. She had never seen her father so speechless.

"Are you all right, Father?"

After a moment, he spoke, "I'm fine, Ana. As I said, you know how I feel. Nevertheless, your mother loved the Lord and loved living her life for Him. I can only imagine how proud she'd be right now. I want to be angry, mind you, but I can't."

By now, Ana was in tears.

"I won't stand in your way, Ana. If this is what you want for your life, then I shall allow it."

"What about Lucy?"

"I won't stand in her way either."

"Thank you, Father."

He gave a weak smile. "I think I will retire off to bed now." He slowly stood with the aid of his crutches.

"Do you need me to help you?"

"No, I can manage. I'm actually getting pretty good at taking care of myself again," he said with a hint of pride.

Ana smiled at him. "Yes, you are, and I am very proud of you, Father."

He gave her another small smile and then was on his way. He stopped at the door and turned around. "I almost forgot. You received a couple of telegrams from Flint

Creek." He pulled the papers from his jacket pocket. Ana rose to retrieve them, and then he continued on his way.

Ana felt completely drained by what had just happened as she sat back down in the chair. Drained but good. She now felt it was possible for her father to come around and find his way back to the Lord. Until a few minutes ago, she had felt it might never happen.

Ana took a deep breath and said a quick prayer of thanks to God. She then opened the first of the telegrams.

> PRAYING FOR JACOB AND CALEB—*stop*—
> THINGS HERE ARE WELL—*stop*—MISS YOU—
> *stop*
>
> JOSIE SCHNIDER

Then the second:

> I GOT SAVED—*stop*—I CAN GO TO HEAVEN
> NOW TOO—*stop*—COME HOME SOON—*stop*
>
> LUCY LAWSON

"Thank You, sweet Heavenly Father! Thank You for saving my Lucy!

The night had finally gotten black enough that Noah, Seth, and Cartwright were all able to sneak down to the farm. They left the rest of their group behind to keep a lookout and moved as quietly as possible. They hadn't seen movement for a couple of hours. Therefore, they felt safe enough to advance at will.

They noticed a young boy several times during the day sneaking from the house to the barn. He always seemed to be carrying something when he went but was always empty-handed when he came back out. They decided, because of this, that the barn was probably the best place to start their search.

The door opened as they arrived alongside the barn, and they all froze behind a stack of crates. Thankfully, the man who stepped out only got a ladle of water from the rain barrel and then went back inside.

The three men exhaled and then crept closer to a window nearer the barn's entrance. From there, they could hear a conversation between two men.

"I can't believe I am finally going to get to meet the boss."

"Yeah. He's done so much for the cause."

"Sure has. I hope he appreciates what we've done too. Surely he is impressed with what we're going to do tomorrow."

"You know he is. I mean, ever since they burned out Latham, he's been in hiding. Now he's risking getting caught just to be here for the hanging."

That last word caused the three men eavesdropping to cringe. The conversation continued. They all leaned in closer, not wanting to miss a word.

"They finished up the gallows this afternoon, so that's all set."

"That's good. I helped to get things ready to cook the hog. They're planning on that going on the spit tomorrow afternoon."

"Um, I cannot wait either! My mouth is already watering!"

"Mine too! Good food *and* a good hanging, all in one day too!"

"Yep, I am looking forward to the food, but what I really can't wait for is watching that *gray scum* in there swing!"

Both men let out a laugh.

"Hey, what's say we get some shut-eye? Those piles of dung ain't goin' anywhere."

"Sounds good to me."

There were a few rustling sounds, and after a few minutes, the men's snores floated through the window.

Even though the fear of being caught sneaking around had diminished somewhat with the sound of the snores, a new fear came flooding in. They now knew the plans for their friends.

Seth led them around the barn in hopes of finding another way in. They stopped dead in their tracks as they rounded the corner, completely taken by surprise by the spectacle before them. Freshly built gallows stood in the center of a large stage. The whole thing had been painted white and had the words "GRAY SCUM MUST DIE!" written in red across the top.

Tables had been set up around the front of it, and a large fire pit and spit were off to the side. To the eye that didn't know better, one would think they were getting ready to have a huge barbeque the whole town was planning to attend.

The sight of it all made Noah ill. He grabbed hold of the barn and closed his eyes, praying for God to take away the sickness. He prayed, most of all, that He would help them get Jacob and Caleb out of this mess. He couldn't bear the thought of what these men here were planning.

Seth touched him on the arm. "You all right?"

"Yes." Noah took a deep breath, chasing the last bit of nausea from his body. "We have to get them away from these people!"

"We will. There's no way I'm going to let this happen," Seth said as he motioned to the horrible sight sprawled out before them.

Little did they know that the two men they were seeking worked feverishly toward the same cause just a few feet away.

Seth, Noah, and Cartwright made their way back to where the rest of their men were waiting. They felt sure Jacob and Caleb were still alive and being held in the barn. They also knew they needed more men and supplies to help with the rescue than what they had with them now. So five or six men headed back to Shreveport for just that.

They spent the next several hours devising a plan of action. They decided it would be best to storm the place under the cover of darkness. This way, they could possibly get all of their men into position before anyone knew they were around.

They worked and planned all through the night and the next day, pausing only to eat and watch the mounting activity at the farm. By afternoon, they were sure the number of men there had reached near fifty. Thankfully, theirs had reached near one hundred. They definitely liked their odds.

Word had reached Ana and James shortly after breakfast that the posse knew where Jacob and Caleb were. They also learned the rescue would occur after nightfall.

"Please let this be it, Lord!" Ana prayed. "Please let this all be over and everyone back here safe and sound come morning!"

Ana had retreated to her room soon after the news arrived. She did her best to concentrate on reading her Bible. Her intent was to search for as much scripture as she could to give her the strength to make it through the day. She paused to ask the Lord for guidance in the Word, and then the scripture began to reveal itself.

Romans chapter 15 and verse 4 reads: "For whatsoever things were written aforetime were written for our learning, that we through patience and comfort of the scriptures might have hope."

Patience—that was exactly what Ana needed! She struggled with being able to turn everything over to the Lord and relinquish the desire to fix it all herself.

Ana also struggled to control her anger. How could someone do such horrible things? First, Liza, and now Jacob and Caleb. These thoughts led to her next verse. Psalms chapter 37, verse 8 and 9 says, "Cease from anger, and forsake wrath: fret not thyself in any wise to do evil. For evildoers shall be cut off: but those that wait upon the Lord, they shall inherit the earth."

Ana vowed to the Lord that she would strive harder to control the anger inside her and to allow Him to handle things. She knew she had to trust in Him more.

Ana had no sooner made her vow than she came across the next passage meant especially for her. It was Psalms chapter 7, verse 1: "O Lord my God, in thee do I put my trust: save me from all them that persecute me, and deliver me."

Then in Psalms chapter 9, verse 10, it says, "And they that know thy name will put their trust in thee: for thou, LORD, hast not forsaken them that seek thee."

Ana hugged her Bible tightly against her chest. "Thank you, sweet Heavenly Father! Thank you for showing Yourself to me here today. I know beyond a shadow of a doubt that You're going to take care of Jacob and Caleb. You said You would, and I humbly put my trust in that truth.

Help us all to stand strong and wait for Your deliverance. Please, Lord, be with Seth, Noah, and the rest of the men. Help them in their quest tonight and keep all involved safe, dear Lord. All these things I ask in Your sweet holy name, amen."

She realized as she dried her tears that a wonderful peace had settled in the room. She knew everything was going to be okay.

It felt like they had been digging for days! However, Jacob and Caleb were finally getting closer. They had started digging up through the ground a few hours ago, but a gnarled mass of tree roots had slowed their progress. Thankfully, they were able to get through the tangled mess. They knew they had to be getting close to breaking through the surface now.

They began to work out a plan for the final stage of their escape while taking a break to eat some of the supper Levi had brought them. They decided to kneel together in a word of prayer once they were satisfied with the idea and had their stomachs full.

"Dear, Heavenly Father," Jacob began, "I pray You will be with us, dear Lord, in the coming hours. Help us, Lord, to be able to break free from this underground prison. Free us from our captures and guide us to safety. Help us, O Lord, to make it back to our loved ones. Be with our loved ones right now, Lord. I know they have to be worried sick about us. Give them peace, dear Lord. All these things we ask in Your name, amen."

In the quiet of the barn, they could hear the faint sounds of the crickets and tree frogs chirping. Nighttime had finally arrived. They also knew this put them closer to the "big event" their captors had planned for them the next day. So they settled back into their routine with a renewed spirit and determination.

29

SETH AND NOAH had spent the afternoon going over the final details of their plan with Capitan Cartwright and the rest of the men. They made sure everyone was on the same page since everything had to go according to the letter of the law.

They began their advance on the farm as soon as the sun went down. Thankfully, they had enough men to surround the whole area, and every angle was covered.

Seth, Noah, and Cartwright moved out ahead of the others. They had made it to the barn and were about to the round the corner when the young boy they had been watching carry in supplies also rounded and ran right into Noah. The boy stumbled backward in shock. Noah had to reach out and grab him to keep him from falling to the ground.

"Who are you?" the young boy's eyes were as big as saucers.

"Not important," Seth told him. "Who are you?"

"Levi…Levi Tate."

"Well, Levi Tate," the captain began, "we have some questions we would like to ask you."

As if running headlong into a tall, muscled-up savage wasn't bad enough, seeing that the soldier addressing him was a Union officer and that the big burly one was wearing a badge, Levi began to shake uncontrollably. He didn't want to get in trouble for what his uncle and the rest had done.

Noah spoke up upon seeing his distress, "Listen, we don't want to hurt you, Levi. We only want to rescue our friends you all have held up in the barn."

"How'd you know?" Levi asked, not even aware he had confirmed what they already knew.

"We've been watching," Noah informed him. "We know you've been sneaking supplies in there to someone. We just assumed it was our friends."

"I didn't want to be a part of all this!" Levi began to cry. "I still don't! I tried to talk them out of it, but they wouldn't listen! I can't bear to think of what they're going to do to those men tomorrow! It just ain't right!"

"Will you help us then?" Noah placed a hand on the young boy's shoulder. "Will you help us get them out of here?"

"I…I…don't know. They'll hang me too if they find out!"

"I promise you they won't do that," Seth reassured him. "We'll make sure of it."

"You don't know who these men are!" Levi protested. "My great uncle is the leader of this mess. He has killed many times and ain't afraid to kill blood kin either."

"We won't let him hurt you, Levi. You have the entire Union army to make sure of that," Cartwright promised.

This seemed to carry some weight, for Levi began to settle down. "What do you want me to do?" He shoved his hands in his pockets.

"Tell us where in the barn they're being held, and then, if you really want out of this mess, make for the tree line. You'll find a group of soldiers there waiting. I'll signal them that you're no threat, and they'll get you to safety."

Levi hung his head. "Sir, it's only me and my kid sister since Ma and Pa passed. If I do this, can you promise you'll take care of us both? 'Cause I know my uncle! He won't think twice about hurting Carrie to get to me."

"As I said before, son," Cartwright began, "you have my word and the word of the entire Union army."

Levi studied him for a moment and then slowly nodded. "They're in the back of the barn, in the tack room. There's a worktable up against the wall. Move it, and you'll see the secret door. Here"—he pulled something from his pocket—"you'll need this." He handed a key over to the captain.

"Do as I told you and head straight for the tree line," Cartwright instructed and then looked in that direction himself and gave a hand signal to the men in the shadows. "Tell them where your sister can be found, and they'll get you both to safety."

Levi nodded again, hesitated briefly, and then took off in a dead run. The three men stood watching, none of them noticing the curtain fall back into place in the second-story window.

"Caleb, I am finally breaking through!" an exhausted Jacob exclaimed.

"Thank God! I am so ready to get out of this hole!"

Jacob finished creating the opening in the ground and slowly stuck his head out and looked around. "The coast is clear. Let's go!"

Ana awoke with a start and then scolded herself for falling asleep. How could she do that? She had to stay awake so she would be ready when they brought Jacob back to her! Ana quickly rose from the chair and began nervously pacing the floor.

A knock at her door caused her to jump. She raced to open it and found her father looking as tense as she felt.

"Have you had a word, Father?"

"No, nothing yet." He looked disappointed that he wasn't able to give her better news. "I couldn't sleep and knew you probably weren't able to either. I thought I would come and keep you company."

"That's a wonderful idea, thank you. Please, come in."

They settled themselves in the living area of Ana's hotel room, and each of them began to fidget. Neither of them seemed to know what to say. The silence seemed to increase, and Ana could take it no longer.

"Father, I know you don't approve—"

"Please, Ana, go ahead and pray." He knew that was where his daughter's heart was.

Ana gave him a tender smile of thanks and then slid off the couch onto the floor and onto her knees. She laid her head across her father's lap and began to pray aloud. She handed everything over to the Lord.

"The Lord is my Shepherd. I shall not want. He maketh me to lie down in green pastures. He leadeth me beside still waters. He restoreth my soul…"

The three men turned and headed for the door of the barn once Levi made it to safety. It struck each of them that it was way too quiet. The crickets had even quieted their song. This caused a new sense of urgency to surge through them. Something wasn't right. They had to get to Jacob and Caleb fast!

They made their way into the barn and headed for the room in the rear where Levi had instructed them to go. Once inside, they saw the worktable and began to slide it out of the way, revealing the trapdoor.

The men all looked at one another and took a deep breath as Seth reached down to remove the lock. They were all shocked when he jerked open the door, revealing an empty pit. Where were they? Noah jumped down into the pit to get a closer look.

Cartwright handed down a lantern. Noah lit it and began to look around. He could tell they had definitely been in there and recently. The remnants of their last meal were on the floor. He turned and saw the hole in the wall of the pit. He peered inside and instantly knew what it was.

"They've escaped," Noah announced to the others. "And not long ago!"

Noah doused the lantern and scrambled to get out of the pit. Seth reached down and, with one quick jerk, had Noah out. The three then left the tack room and headed for the front door.

Cartwright took a quick peek outside and then turned to the others to declare the way clear. Just as he took his first step out of the door, gunshots rang out. A bullet hit him in the shoulder, knocking him back against the barn door. Seth reached to grab him and pulled him back into the safety of the barn.

The whole world seemed to explode around them. Gunshots rang out from every direction. They knew they had them outnumbered and that it would be only a matter of time before this would all be over. Even then, the question remained. Where were Jacob and Caleb?

"Gunfire!" Caleb exclaimed as he finished climbing out of the dark tunnel.

"They've figured us out!" Jacob helped his friend to his feet. "We have to get out of here! Run, Caleb!"

The two men took off as fast as their feet could carry them. They didn't get very far, however, before they found themselves surrounded by Union soldiers. All of them with guns drawn.

"State your name!" one of them ordered.

"I'm Sergeant Jacob Dalton with the Confederate Army."

"And I'm Corporal Caleb Johnson with the Confederate Army. What are y'all doing here?"

"Looking for you," the soldier said smugly as he lowered his weapon.

Jacob and Caleb watched as the rest of the men did the same.

"He leadeth me in the paths of righteousness for His name' sake. Yea, though I walk through the valley of the shadow of death, I will fear no evil, for thou art with me..."

"So Noah, Seth, and your captain are down there in the middle of all that chaos?" Jacob asked for clarification as the sounds of the fighting grew heavier down around the barn.

"Yes, and we fear the captain has been shot."

"What about the other two?" Jacob grew more worried for his friends by the second.

"We don't know. We were headed in to help when we saw you."

Jacob and Caleb looked at each other and silently agreed on their next step.

"Give us some guns," Jacob ordered. "We're going with you."

"Can't do that, sir. The captain would want us to get you two to safety."

"We're the reason you boys are here at all, and we're not about to sit around and do nothing," Jacob informed him. "Now, please, give us some guns."

"The wound doesn't look too bad. Looks like the bullet went straight through," Noah told Cartwright as he finished with his makeshift bandage of corn husks and twine, which he had found in the crib.

"Thank you, Noah."

"You're welcome. Now, what do you say we see about getting out of here without any more wounds to patch?"

"Sounds like a plan to me." Cartwright grunted as Noah helped him to his feet.

They made their way over to where Seth was firing off shots through an open window.

"I can see the reinforcements moving in." Seth pulled back away from the window to reload his Remington nickel revolver.

"Wonderful news!" Cartwright exclaimed as he began taking aim through another window.

Noah gathered up his pistols and rifle and made a check of the barn to make sure no one had come in through another entrance. Thankfully, everyone seemed to be concentrating on the front of the barn. Noah saw no signs of anyone, except for the reinforcements they had brought with them beginning to close in. He decided to head back up front to help Seth and Cartwright.

Seth announced as he reached the front of the barn, "That's him! That's the sorry piece of horse dung that leads this outfit!"

"Where?" Cartwright asked and then began peering through the crack Seth had been looking through.

"Second-floor balcony."

Noah and Cartwright both looked in that direction and saw a distinguished middle-aged man hiding behind a tall plant, watching the mayhem below.

"We have to get that bast—," Seth started.

"You are absolutely right!" Noah took aim with his long-range rifle.

He wasn't able to get the shot off, however. Someone came from the shadows behind them as he was about to pull the trigger.

"Thy rod and thy staff, they comfort me. Thou preparest a table before me in the presence of mine enemies. Thou annointest my head with oil. My cup runneth over…"

"Jacob!" Noah and Seth yelled in unison.

"Thank God you're all right!" Noah gave his friend a big hug.

"Thank God that you are!" Jacob laughed and then shook Seth's awaiting hand.

"We didn't know what to think when that pit back there was empty," Seth admitted.

"Imagine our surprise, as we ran for our lives, running headlong into a line of Union soldiers! Guys, this here is Caleb Johnson," Jacob replied.

Seth introduced Captain Cartwright, and everyone began to shake hands. Suddenly a bullet came through the window, zoomed right past Caleb's head, and splintered a wooden post behind him.

"Uh, fellas—I think we need to get our attention back to what's going on out there," Caleb said as he unholstered his Colt .44 and headed for the front wall.

The others followed suit. In no time, their men gained control of the situation.

Gunfire became sporadic and mostly in the woods and fields surrounding the house and barn. They could see the coast was clear enough for them to venture out of their refuge. They began to help secure the prisoners and ready them for transport. In the midst of this, Jacob remembered Levi.

"Seth, there was a young boy—," Jacob began.

"Levi. Yes, he's safe. He helped us to find you."

"Good." Jacob was relieved. "He's a good kid. Just mixed up in a bad situation."

"Yep, I agree," Seth offered, and they went back to work.

A single shot pierced the night air as they were loading the last of the men onto the buckboard. Another shot quickly followed.

"Surely goodness and mercy shall follow me all the days of my life, and I will dwell in the House of the Lord forever."

Amen.

EPILOGUE

"Ana, get a move on! You're going to make us all late for church!" Lucy fussed from her position in the bedroom door.

Ana had been sitting at her dressing table staring in the mirror for quite a while. She was reliving the night Noah and Seth had gone to rescue Jacob and Caleb. It was hard for her to believe it had been almost a year ago.

Ana sat and recalled the story the men told her once they had returned. A shiver ran through her body, chilling her from head to toe, as she remembered their plan for Jacob and Caleb! She couldn't believe they were actually going to hang them and then celebrate it with a huge feast!

She thought about the gun battle they fought and the petrifying tells of the final shots that rang out. It was such a horribly stressful time for all involved.

"Ana!" Lucy called from the bottom of the stairs.

"I'll only be a few more minutes."

"Well, hurry up! Thomas already has the wagon out front."

"All right!" Ana hoped Lucy would leave her to her thoughts for a little while longer.

Things back at the ranch had changed quite a bit since then. Ana walked over and looked out the side window of her room and down at the activity of the ranch below. She marveled at how everything worked like a well-oiled machine and realized that was probably the only thing that hadn't changed.

She watched as Lucy chased Bandit across the yard. She found it amazing how one year could make such a difference in a child. Lucy was still the same tomboyish little girl she had always been. However, she was getting more independent and helped Josie around the ranch a lot more. She had made so many new friends and seemed happier than Ana had ever seen her. Of course, Ana truly believed it had more to do with her salvation and devotion to the Lord than anything else.

Josie and Thomas still acted as if they were newlyweds and had even become parents! They had happily adopted Levi—the little boy who helped Noah and Seth locate Jacob and Caleb—and his sister, Carrie.

The kids were doing great! They had adjusted wonderfully to life on the ranch and life in Flint Creek in general. The Lord saved Levi not long after they came to the ranch. Carrie was only five, so she probably wasn't ready for that. She loved going to church and learning about Jesus, though.

Everyone else on the ranch was also doing well. Noah and Beth were expecting another little one in a few months! Isaiah was growing so fast! He was also looking forward to being a big brother.

Ana's father, James, had officially moved to Flint Creek. Thankfully, he had recovered wonderfully from his injuries. The doctors were able to construct him an artificial, leg and he could maneuver around with it rather well. He wasn't able to get around quickly, but he was extremely thankful to be getting around at all.

Ana believed his happiness had less to do with his recovery and more to do with Katie's mother, Nancy. Ana never dreamed she would ever see her father with another woman. However, as she watched them walk hand in hand down the lane toward the newly erected Cowboy Church, Ana was so happy for them she could burst!

Ana had so hoped Caleb would have come back to Flint Creek so he and Katie could have met. Unfortunately, Caleb decided right away he was not finished with serving his country.

Ana felt her life had changed the most. She started working in town for Doc Swenson after recovering from her last ordeal in Shreveport. She loved it so much she had decided to get her official training to become a nurse. She planned to start on that in a few months' time.

"Ana Grace! You can stare out the window after church!" Lucy called up to her from below.

"I'm coming, Lucy! It's just now time to be leaving anyway!" Ana decided her daydreaming would have to be over for the time being. She stood to leave and found Josie standing in the doorway with a smile on her face.

"What?" Ana asked innocently.

Josie chuckled. "You can't fault her on her zeal to be at church."

"No, you can't. That's for sure."

"Are you all right, Ana? You're losing yourself in your thoughts a lot lately."

"I've been thinking a lot about the past year and how so much has changed."

"It has indeed." Josie placed her hands on her niece's shoulders and looked her in the eyes. "Ana, I am so proud of how far you have come. I know your mother would be as well. You have endured so much, yet despite that—or maybe because of that—you have grown into an amazing young woman."

"Oh, Josie!" Ana grabbed her in a hug. "Thanks for everything you have done for me these past couple of years. You will never know how much it means to me."

They heard the front door open and the sounds of Lucy stomping toward the stairs. Ana and Josie laughed.

"We had better go."

"Yes, we had." Josie gave another chuckle.

They then headed out the door and down the stairs, meeting Lucy halfway.

"It's about time!" Lucy huffed, spun around, and headed back down the stairs and toward the door. Ana and Josie exchanged amused looks and continued out themselves.

Josie went on ahead, and Ana hesitated on the top step. She looked at the scene in front of her and again marveled at how much her life had changed. Lucy was already giving her a hateful look, so she took a deep breath and walked on to the wagon. She paused once again when she reached the side.

"You better hurry up and let me help you get up there, or she might actually explode."

"I'm not afraid of her," Ana said with mock defiance. "Or you either, Mr. Dalton."

"You better be, Mrs. Dalton." Jacob gave one of his famous grins. "Ain't that right, little one?" he asked as he patted his wife's expanding tummy.

CPSIA information can be obtained
at www.ICGtesting.com
Printed in the USA
LVOW12s0004160916
504815LV00013B/53/P

9 781682 707678

A Heart's Journey